# THE PLAY OF

# Goggle Eyes

## ANNE FINE

**Questions and activities by Alison Jenkins**

**Series editor: Lawrence Till**

Heinemann Educational,
a division of Heinemann Publishers (Oxford) Ltd
Halley Court, Jordan Hill, Oxford OX2 8EJ

OXFORD   LONDON   EDINBURGH
MADRID   ATHENS   BOLOGNA   PARIS
MELBOURNE   SYDNEY   AUCKLAND   SINGAPORE   TOKYO
IBADAN   NAIROBI   HARARE   GABORONE   PORTSMOUTH NH (USA)

First published in the *Heinemann Plays* series 1995
95 96 97 98 10 9 8 7 6 5 4 3 2 1

A catalogue record for this book is available from the British Library on request.
ISBN 0 435 23309 2

Cover design by Keith Pointing

Original design by Jeffery White Creative Associates; adapted by Jim Turner

Typeset by CentraCet Limited, Cambridge

Printed by Clays Ltd, St Ives plc

*Goggle-Eyes* was first published as a novel by Hamish Hamilton Children's Books in 1989, and is available in Puffin. The television serial in four episodes, adapted by Deborah Moggach, was first shown by the BBC in 1993.

# CONTENTS

# INTRODUCTION

Since its publication in 1989, Anne Fine's story *Goggle-Eyes* has become one of the most popular novels for young people. It was winner of the Guardian Children's Fiction Award and the Carnegie Medal. It has also been dramatized for television.

Ann Fine wrote this stage-play version of *Goggle-Eyes* specially for the Heinemann Play Series.

*Goggle-Eyes* is the story of Kitty, a headstrong, confident girl, and her sister, Jude, who live with their mother. Since her divorce their Mum has had a number of relationships, none of which has been important enough to interfere in the lives of the Killin family. Then Gerald, otherwise known as Goggle-eyes, arrives. Gerald is as conventional as Mum is unorthodox and as organized as she is chaotic. Kitty can't understand why her Mum is attracted to this man who doesn't care about the environment and who looks at the world as though he is looking at a business plan. However, it seems Goggle-eyes has come to stay. The play explores how the relationships between the characters change and develop.

You will find suggestions for follow-up work at the end of the play. The first section, **Keeping Track**, comprises straightforward questions on the text to help you consider in more depth what is happening in the play. Ideas for a more detailed look at the issues raised in the play can be found in the **Explorations** section.

# About the Author

'Anne Fine writes with wit and ingenuity, her characters are lively and the dialogue sparkles.'

*Signal Review*

'A writer of great originality, Anne Fine's books are a true delight to read.'

*Children's Fiction Sourcebook*

'Anne Fine has a well developed and delicious sense of humour, a remarkable ear for dialogue, and a robust but sympathetic attitude towards family disasters.'

*Scotland on Sunday*

Anne Fine is one of Britain's most popular and prestigious writers for young people. Amongst the many awards she has won are the Carnegie Medal, once for *Goggle-Eyes* and once for *Flour Babies*; the Guardian Children's Fiction Award for *Goggle-Eyes*; a Smarties Prize for *Bill's New Frock*; and the Whitbread Children's Novel Award. In 1990 and 1993 she was Children's Writer of the Year. She has written twenty-five books, for both adults and children, and been translated into twenty languages. *Goggle-Eyes* was screened by the BBC in four episodes, and her novel *Madame Doubtfire* has been filmed by Twentieth-Century-Fox, starring Robin Williams.

Anne Fine was born in Leicester and has lived both in Canada and the United States. She has two grown-up daughters and now lives in County Durham.

# List of Characters

**Kitty**  is a lively, outspoken girl of secondary-school age, keen on green issues, and very much more powerful than her sister –

**Jude**  who is several years younger, quieter and gentler, and occasionally still sucks her thumb.

**Mum**  is cheerful and busy. She has a full-time job at the hospital, but still manages to go to meetings and get involved in local issues. The only thing she doesn't have time to do is tidy the house.

**Gerald**  is Mum's new boyfriend. He's middle-aged and balding, and he runs a small printing firm.

**Mrs Harrison**  is far too old to babysit any more. She tends to shuffle round the house, talking to herself.

**Beth**  runs the group concerned with green issues to which Mum and Kitty belong. She is an earth-mother type, and walks around with outlandish banners, clothes and food.

**Flossie**  is the cat: a huge, malevolent-looking ball of fur. Though unashamedly stuffed, all characters treat Flossie at all times as if she were alive.

# GOGGLE-EYES

## Act One

*Kitty speaks to the audience.*

**Kitty**  You can't help how you feel. I know it would be simpler all round if, when your Mum and Dad said, 'I'm sorry, but we're splitting up,' you could just shrug and not mind. If you could get used to it easily, just to suit them. But getting used to things isn't that quick and easy. Mind you, we weren't doing that badly . . .

## Scene One

*Mum's bedroom.*

*The room is comfy but cluttered. There are Greenpeace posters above the desk. A 'Save the Whales' banner leans against the wall. Mum is nailing an 'Only One Earth' sign to a broom handle which Jude is suposed to be holding steady. But Jude keeps glancing at the television which is playing softly in the corner.*

**Mum**  Jude, hold it still.

**Jude**  I am.

**Mum**  No, you're not. It keeps slipping. Watch what you're doing.

**Jude**  I am.

**Mum**  No, you're not. You've got your eyes on that telly.

**Jude**  No, I haven't. Oh! Quick, Mum! It's starting!

**Mum**  See?

**Jude**      Kitty! Kitty! Come in here. It's starting!

*Jude jumps up on the bed.*

Come on, Mum. Leave all that.

*Mum lays down the hammer, and climbs on the bed beside Jude.*

**Mum**      Hotch up. You're taking all the room.

**Jude**      Kitty! Hurry up! You'll miss it!

**Kitty**     No, I won't. Are we on the right channel?

**Jude**      'Course we are. Sssh!

**Kitty**     Did you get the posters finished, ready for the meeting tonight?

**Mum**      'Course I did. Sssh!

**Kitty**     Does anyone want a banana?

**Mum**      ⎫
            ⎬  Sssh!
**Jude**     ⎭

*We hear the signature tune of a popular soap opera. Kitty hands round bananas.*

**Kitty**     I can't believe she's going to marry him. He's such a slimy creep.

**Mum**      ⎫
            ⎬  Sssh!
**Jude**     ⎭

*The phone rings.*

**Kitty**     Just leave it.

**Jude**      Yes, leave it. Whoever it is can ring back later.

*Mum leaps off the bed.*

**Mum**      No, I'll get it.

*She lifts the phone, and carries it to the limit of its wire, just out of sight in the doorway, before lifting the receiver.*

*Kitty turns to Jude.*

**Kitty**     Now that's not like Mum.

**Jude**      Maybe she knows who's ringing.

**Kitty**     I can't think of anyone she'd miss her serial to talk to.

*Kitty turns down the television sound. Together they eavesdrop.*

*From offstage.*

**Mum**   Oh, goody! It *is* you. I thought it might be.

*Kitty and Jude exchange a look of surprise.*

*From offstage.*

**Mum**   Oh, no. I can't come tonight. I have to go to a meeting with Kitty.

**Jude**   Who's inviting Mum out tonight? Is it Gran, do you think?

*From offstage.*

**Mum**   No. Kitty's the *older* one. It's Jude who's the baby.

**Jude**   Cheek!

**Kitty**   So it's not Gran. Or Dad. Or any of her friends. It's someone new. Who is it?

*From offstage.*

**Mum**   Take me where? Oh, Gerald! I'd love to. I've been wanting to go there for ages.

**Kitty**   Gerald?

**Jude**   Gerald?

*From offstage.*

**Mum**   All right, then. I can't say no. I'll fix it up with Kitty just this once.

**Kitty**   Oh, will you?

**Jude**   Who's this Gerald, Kitty?

**Kitty**   How on earth should I know? I've never heard of any Gerald. I remember Simon.

**Jude**   Oh, I loved Simon. He always helped me with my maths.

**Kitty**   And I remember Colin.

**Jude**   He was wet.

**Kitty**   And I remember Paul.

**Jude**   Paul didn't last long.

| | |
|---|---|
| **Kitty** | But never Gerald. I've never heard of Gerald. |
| | *Mum comes back in, and starts to haul clothes out of drawers and closets.* |
| **Mum** | What am I going to wear? |
| | *Kitty pretends to misunderstand.* |
| **Kitty** | Jeans and a woolly are just fine for the meeting, Mum. It's what you always wear. |
| **Mum** | Oh, Kitty. You're going to have to let me off the meeting, just this once. I'm going to 'Le Chat Noir'. |
| **Jude** | What's that? |
| | *Mum pulls on fancy clothes, inspects herself in the mirror as they speak, then tears them off and tries others.* |
| **Mum** | It's that posh French restaurant next to the Town Hall. |
| **Kitty** | I see. You're going to let the whales and dolphins stick up for themselves, while you eat pâté de foie gras? You're going to let this poor old planet care for itself, while you eat baby veal? You're going to let pollution take over, while you – |
| **Mum** | Kitty! It's only this once! Can't I go out just once in a blue moon? |
| **Jude** | But you'll be ages. And you said you'd help me with my project tonight, when you and Kitty got back. I've still got tons of it to make. |
| | *Mum is putting on lipstick.* |
| **Mum** | I'm sure Mrs Harrison will help you with it while she's babysitting. |
| **Jude** | Oh, Mum! She'll ruin it! She's so old she can hardly see! |
| | *The doorbell rings.* |
| **Mum** | Ssh! She'll hear you. |
| **Kitty** | Fat chance! She's not just half blind, you know. She's practically stone deaf as well. |
| **Mum** | Kitty! |
| | *Mum turns to Jude.* |

Quick, Jude. Don't keep her waiting on the doorstep. Go and let her in.

*Jude leaves the room.*

**Kitty**  Well, Mrs Harrison's not babysitting me. I'm going to the meeting. And I'm going now. So you're going to have to choose. Are you going to keep your only once-a-week date with me – your only get-to-be-with-Kitty-by-herself time? Or are you tarting yourself up like a Barbie-doll to go out with some stupid fat stranger called Gerald you've only just met?

*Mum narrows her eyes threateningly at Kitty.*

**Mum**  I certainly hope you're going to be a whole lot more polite than that when you meet him.

**Kitty**  Oh, do you? Well, we'll see!

*Kitty slams out.*

*Mum picks up a fancy jacket.*

**Mum**  Yes, I most certainly do! And, yes, we will!

*Mum slams out after Kitty.*

*The television is left flickering mournfully in an empty room.*

## Scene Two

*Downstairs.*

*The open-plan ground floor of the Killin household. We can see the kitchen area, and the way off, or up, to Mum's bedroom. Jude is on the sofa, looking excited, and studying her watch every few seconds. Kitty is standing to the side, unnoticed until she speaks.*

*Kitty addresses the audience.*

**Kitty**  I know a storm warning when I hear one. So when we finally got to meet this famous Gerald – Mr Gerald

Faulkner – exactly a week later, I made sure there was nothing she could pin on me in the bad manners line. After all, there's nothing rude about only speaking when you're spoken to, is there? And nothing rude about standing quietly in the background when someone rings the doorbell, and not being the first one to rush across and let them in.

*The doorbell rings.*

*Jude rushes to open it.*

*Mum appears, half-dressed, in her doorway.*

**Mum**    Jude! Kitty! Get the door, will you?

**Jude**    I *am*.

**Kitty**    (*softly*) I'm *not*.

*Jude opens the door to Gerald, hidden behind a huge bunch of flowers and a box of chocolates. He hands the chocolates to Jude.*

**Gerald**    Hello. You must be Judith.

**Jude**    That's right. Are these for Mum?

**Gerald**    The flowers are. The chocolates are for you –

*He catches sight of Kitty.*

– both.

*Kitty scowls and turns her face away.*
*Gerald picks up Flossie the cat, and strokes her while keeping his eyes on Kitty.*

**Gerald**    Purrr. Purrr. Who's a *nice* Kitty?

*Kitty turns her back on Gerald.*

**Jude**    Mum says to get yourself a drink. She's almost ready.

**Gerald**    Righty-ho.

*He goes directly to the cabinet with the glasses, then the cupboard with the lemons. He starts to mix four complicated, ice-tinkling drinks. Kitty pulls her sister away, to whisper.*

**Kitty**    Jude! Jude! He's been here before. He knows exactly where everything is. He must have been here when we've been out at school. Or fast asleep.

| | |
|---|---|
| **Jude** | What does it matter? |
| **Kitty** | It just does. |
| **Jude** | I don't see why. |
| **Kitty** | Well, maybe you're stupid. |
| **Jude** | There's no need to be horrible. |

*Mum overhears the last of this as she sails in wearing a frilly blouse and velvet slacks.*

**Mum**     Who's being horrible?

*Gerald turns round fast. He's clearly been listening, but now wants to distract Mum.*

**Gerald**   Oh, Rosalind! You look lovely!

**Kitty**     Mum is called Rosie. You'd better get her name right if you're going on a date.

**Mum**     Kitty, your sister's quite right. There's no need to be horrible.

*Mum turns to Gerald.*

You mustn't mind Kitty. She's just in a mood because it's the second time in a row that I'm skipping our meeting to go out with you.

**Gerald**   Meeting? What meeting?

**Mum**     'Protect the Planet.' We meet every week.

**Kitty**     *Some* of us . . .

**Gerald**   And what do you do at these meetings?

**Mum**     Kitty will tell you. I just have to nip upstairs again. The buckle's broken on this belt.

**Gerald**   Rosalind –

*Mum turns back.*

**Mum**     Yes?

**Gerald**   I said you looked lovely. And it's absolutely true. But won't you spoil me a little? Wear the blue top with all the fiddly little buttons, and the black skirt with diamond stockings, and the shiny bow shoes.

*Mum smiles, then runs back upstairs.*
*Gerald stands watching her.*
*Kitty pulls Jude aside again, to whisper.*

**Kitty**   What *is* this guy? Is he some *wardrobe* pervert?

**Jude**   I can't remember Dad ever asking Mum to go back up and change into something he liked better.

**Kitty**   And, if he had, Mum would have had more sense than to trot back like a trained Barbie-doll, and do it.

**Jude**   I think it's *nice*.

**Kitty**   I think it's *stupid*.

*Gerald turns his attention back to them.*

**Gerald**   Lucky for me that this is Request Night, eh, girls?

*He hands round the drinks he's made.*

And cocktail time. This one is yours, Judith. And, Kitty, this one is yours. I didn't put any alcohol in it because I didn't know if you liked the taste.

*Kitty looks astonished, and a bit pleased.*

**Jude**   Good job Mum didn't hear you say that.

**Gerald**   Why?

**Jude**   She thinks that Kitty's only ever tasted lemonade.

**Gerald**   Hasn't she noticed Kitty's practically grown up?

**Jude**   Practically grown up? Kitty?

**Gerald**   She looks pretty grown up to me. Old enough to go off to meetings on her own. Old enough to have her own views.

*He settles himself on the sofa. Jude settles easily at his side, and interests herself quietly in the chocolates.*

And old enough to explain them.

*Kitty scowls and looks away.*

**Gerald**   Well, go on, then.

**Kitty**   What?

**Gerald**   Explain them.

**Kitty**   Explain what?

| | |
|---|---|
| **Gerald** | All this 'Protect the Planet' stuff. What is your group trying to do? Get all the furry and feathery creatures out of their cages? Stop everyone building new motorways? Get the nuclear power stations closed? Save the whales? Shut the weapons factories? |
| **Kitty** | (*icily*) Those sorts of things, yes. |
| **Gerald** | You can't stop progress, though. Take nuclear power, for example. It's been invented now. You can't just pretend that it hasn't. You can't disinvent it. |
| **Kitty** | You can't disinvent thumb screws, either. Or gas chambers. But you can dismantle them. And you should. |
| **Gerald** | All I'm trying to say is, the better the weapon, the better the defence. |
| **Kitty** | That's silly. Half of these brilliant weapons are so brilliant they can't be used. A weapon that poisons the planet you live on can't defend you, can it? You can't even use it. It would just be suicide. |
| **Gerald** | But that's the point. The chances are that you won't have to use them. Just having them in the background keeps the peace. |
| **Kitty** | Oh, yes? Like some people smoke cigarettes year after year with lung cancer in the background? They might not have it now. But they might get it next week. Or the week after. What sort of peace do you call that? |
| **Gerald** | Good enough for someone like me. |
| **Kitty** | Someone as *old* as you, perhaps you mean. |
| | *Jude looks up, shocked.* |
| **Jude** | Kitty! |
| **Kitty** | No, I mean it. And it's a bit selfish not to be bothered about what happens to the planet, just because you won't be on it very much longer. |
| **Gerald** | You probably forget that someone as ancient as me is old enough to know about other times. Times when bombs weren't as terrible as they are now, so |

countries didn't have to be so careful not to start huge international wars. Times when, in almost every city in Europe, orphans were picking their way through piles of smoking rubble.

*Jude looks up from the chocolate box.*

**Jude**   Were things really like that?

**Gerald**   Yes, they were.

**Kitty**   I shouldn't look so worried, Jude. Mr Faulkner's family probably didn't have too bad a time in the war.

**Gerald**   Quite a few of my family were killed in it. Will that do?

**Jude**   (*horrified*) Quite a few?

**Gerald**   Yes. Quite a few.

**Kitty**   Then I'm surprised you're not a bit keener to stop the people who build these huge weapon factories. After all, look what they do. First they make great fortunes selling these horrible weapons of theirs all over the world. And then they just sit back and weep crocodile tears when 'quite a few' die in other people's families.

**Gerald**   It's not as simple as that. Of course I'd prefer it if there were no weapon factories. Anybody would. But if people are going to buy them, then people are going to make them.

**Kitty**   Try looking at it the other way. If people are going to make them, then people are going to buy them.

**Gerald**   Well, jobs are important.

**Kitty**   Not that important.

**Gerald**   They are if you're not lucky enough to have one.

*Mum comes back, dressed as requested in a skirt and the top with the fiddly buttons.*

**Mum**   Lucky enough to have what?

**Gerald**   A job.

**Mum**   Jobs! Don't talk to me about jobs! Today, at the hospital, we ran out of disinfectant. Can you believe that? In a hospital? One of the staff opened her cupboard, and it was practically bare. Of course, she phoned me up at once, and –

*Distracted, Mum leans forward and peers in the mirror.*

Have I done all these fiddly little buttons up wrong? I have! No wonder I hardly ever wear this! I've got to unbutton the whole lot, and start again.

**Gerald**   Judith will help you. She's got little fingers.

**Kitty**   Her name is Jude.

**Jude**   No, really, Kitty. It's all right. I like Judith. No one has ever called me Judith before.

*Kitty hisses at her sister.*

**Kitty**   Oh, fine. Take his side.

**Jude**   I'm not taking sides!

**Gerald**   Just help your mother with her little buttons, Judith. Or we'll be late.

**Mum**   It's all right. I can see what I'm doing.

*Mum rises on tiptoe to see the reflection of the top in the mirror. Her skirt rides up.*

**Kitty**   What are you staring at?

**Gerald**   (*reprovingly*) I'm not *staring*, Kitty. I'm *looking*. In fact, I'm *admiring*. I'm admiring your mother's good looks.

**Kitty**   (*under her breath*) I bet you mean her *legs*.

**Mum**   (*overhearing*) Legs? Is there something wrong with my legs now?

*She stares down in despair.*

Oh, dear. I'm dead fed up with my body.

**Gerald**   Give it to me, then.

*Mum laughs.*

*It's the last straw. Kitty explodes.*

**Kitty**   Shut up! Stop staring at her, and shut up!

**Mum**   Kitty, it was a *joke*. It was just a *joke*.

**Kitty**   Well, it wasn't funny! And what is he doing in here
            anyway? Nobody wants him! He's nothing but a
            Peeping Tom! He's a dirty old man, forcing you
            upstairs to put on different clothes, so he can stare at
            you better! He's a horrid creepy Goggle-eyes!

**Mum**    Kitty! How *dare* you?

**Kitty**   How *dare* I? What about *him*? How dare *he*? Horrid
            creepy Goggle-eyes!

            *Everyone is staring in horror at Kitty, who suddenly
            realizes what she has said, bursts into tears, and
            rushes from the room.*
            *Judith has shrunk into the sofa. Mum and Gerald
            stare miserably at one another.*
            *Upstairs, a door slams, hard.*

## Scene Three

*Downstairs.*

*It is three weeks later. Every possible light and lamp
is blazing away. Mrs Harrison is shuffling towards the
television room with Flossie the cat tucked under her
arm. Kitty is behind her, silently doing an imitation of
her walk and speech.*

**Mrs Harrison**   So I said to her, 'You stick to your favourite way of
            roasting a chicken, dear. And I'll stick to mine.' Are
            those my spectacles? Oh, no. It's one of Jude's little
            home-made metal sheep. I haven't missed it yet, have
            I, dear? You've put me on the right channel?

**Kitty**   Yes, I've put you on the right channel. And there's
            your glasses. In your hand.

**Mrs Harrison**   Oh, yes, dear.

            *Kitty begins to imitate her behind her back again.*
            So I said to her, I just told her straight, 'Some people
            like a lemon stuck in it, and garlic rubbed all over.
            And other people like it plain. And I like it plain.'

*Though still imitating Mrs Harrison, Kitty is falling further and further behind.*

And guess what she said to me? Guess! The cheeky little madam. She said, 'Not so much plain as downright overcooked, if you want my opinion. This chicken's not just falling off the bone. It's melting into the gravy.' What a cheek!

*Mrs Harrison disappears from sight. Kitty snaps into her normal self, gathers a pile of papers and a pen, and sits at the table. She studies the titles set for her homework essays, thinking hard.*

**Kitty**  Essay for tomorrow morning. Which one shall I choose?

*From offstage.*

**Mrs Harrison**  So I said to her, 'No call for that sort of rudeness, dear. Especially not under my roof.

*The voice is fading.*

I'll thank you to keep a civil tongue in your head while you've got your feet under my table. And why that son of mine puts up with . . .'

**Kitty**  'A Sudden Windfall.' 'First Trip Abroad.' 'Something I Hate.'

*She laughs.*

Oh, yes! Brilliant! 'Something I Hate.' Oh, yes, indeed!

*She starts to write furiously.*
*Jude bursts in, waving her homework book.*

**Jude**  Mum! Mum! Look at this! Mum!

*Kitty keeps writing.*

**Kitty**  She's not here.

**Jude**  Oh, poke! Where is she?

**Kitty**  (*sarcastically*) Where do you think?

**Jude**  Oh, not again! This is the third time this week.

**Kitty**  Fourth.

*Jude hurls the homework book down. Kitty keeps writing.*

**Jude**  Who's sitting for us?

**Kitty**  Guess.

**Jude**  Oh, no. Not again. Where is she?

**Kitty**  She's upstairs, chuntering to herself in front of the telly.

**Jude**  Why?

*Kitty finishes the first sheet, and whips out another. Still without looking up, she carries on writing.*

**Kitty**  I don't think she's noticed I'm not there.

**Jude**  Mum shouldn't leave us with her all the time!

**Kitty**  I must say, I can't see the point. If there was ever a fire, the two of us would be burned to a crisp while we helped Mrs Harrison look for her glasses so she could get down the stairs.

**Jude**  (*cheering up*) Never mind. Maybe Mum will be back soon.

**Kitty**  (*bitterly*) With Goggle-eyes.

**Jude**  You shouldn't call him that.

**Kitty**  I'll call him what I like.

**Jude**  Look at the trouble you got in last time. Mum said you ruined their evening.

*Kitty looks up for the first time.*

**Kitty**  Did she?

**Jude**  Yes.

**Kitty**  Good.

*She bends her head back to her work again.*

**Jude**  She said that the restaurant Gerald took her to cost the earth, and both of them were so upset that everything ended up tasting of carpet.

**Kitty**  Good. Pity he didn't choke to death on some of it.

**Jude**  Kitty! You shouldn't say things like that.

**Kitty**  Like what?

**Jude**  You know. Wishing people dead.

*Kitty puts down her pen. She advances on Jude, who keeps stepping backwards.*

**Kitty** Shouldn't I? Really? You mean it would be wrong of me to say I'd like a chimney to fall on his head and brain him?

**Jude** Kitt-ee!

*Kitty is still advancing.*

**Kitty** Or for him to stumble down the side of the canal, and drown.

**Jude** Kitt-ee!

**Kitty** Or drop his electric heater in the bath, and fry!

*Jude claps her hands over her ears.*

Or trip and fall on his best carving knife.

*Kitty pulls Jude's hands away from her ears.*

Or mix his beer up with a jar of rat poison, and drink the wrong one.

**Jude** Kitty! Stop! Please stop!

**Kitty** Why should I? Give me one reason why I should.

**Jude** Because I *like* him. That's why.

*Kitty steps back in astonishment.*

**Kitty** You *like* him? How can you *like* him?

*Jude is clearly embarrassed.*

**Jude** I just do.

**Kitty** How? *Why?*

**Jude** I don't know. I just do. He's nice to me. He makes me laugh. And he makes Mum laugh, too. And he helps me for hours with my horrible homework. And he reads to me.

**Kitty** The stock market reports! He reads the stock market reports aloud to you while you sit on his knee!

**Jude** Well, I like listening to them.

**Kitty** You just like being cuddled!

**Jude** So?

**Kitty**   It doesn't count. It's just because you're missing Dad.

**Jude**    It's not! That's not fair! You can like two people in the whole wide world!

**Kitty**   Well, I don't like Goggle-eyes. Not one bit.

*She waves the essay she's been writing in the air.*

And everyone at school is going to know how much I hate him.

**Jude**    Why? What's that?

**Kitty**   It's just an essay. Called 'Something I Hate.'

**Jude**    Kitty, that's *mean*.

*Kitty jumps on a chair, and reads aloud.*

**Kitty**   'Something I hate comes round to our house practically every day now. Slimy and creepy and revolting, it makes me absolutely sick. It walks in here and acts as if it owns the place. The first thing it does is switch off all the lights it thinks we don't need. "There!" it says. "That should slow the little electric wheel down to a sprint!" Then it starts goggling at Mum, and telling her what to wear. And Mum's so wrapped up in this new thing of hers that she doesn't even notice that – '

*Kitty breaks off.*

What's that?

**Jude**    What?

**Kitty**   That noise.

**Jude**    It's them! They're back!

*Jude snatches up her homework book and rushes to greet them. Hastily, Kitty slides her essay out of sight under a newspaper on the table. Gerald walks in, followed by Mum.*

**Gerald**  Hello, Kitty.

**Kitty**   (*sourly*) Hello again.

**Jude**    Mum! Look at this! I got a tick for all the homework Gerald did with me.

*Gerald walks round the room, switching off all the unnecessary lights.*

**Mum** That's wonderful, Jude! Well done!

**Gerald** There! That should slow the little electric wheel down to a sprint.

*Kitty raises her eyes to heaven.*

**Mum** Did you hear that, Gerald? You and Jude have done very well indeed at school today.

**Gerald** Oh, goody!

**Kitty** Oh, for heaven's sake!

*Kitty turns away. Gerald shrugs his shoulders at her back, then whips out a box of chocolates.*

**Gerald** We've earned these, then, Jude.

*He walks across to Kitty.*

Would you like one, Kitty?

**Kitty** (*sourly*) No, thanks.

**Jude** But they're your favourites, Kitty!

*Kitty narrows her eyes at Jude.*

**Kitty** I said, 'No, thanks!'

*Mrs Harrison wanders in.*

**Mrs Harrison** Ooh, chocolates! Lovely.

**Gerald** Do have one, Mrs Harrison.

**Mrs Harrison** I won't say no.

**Gerald** In fact, have two. Have yours and Kitty's. She's not having any.

**Mrs Harrison** Aren't you, dear? I thought these were your favourites.

*Kitty scowls horribly.*

Well, I won't say no. I'll have this one.

*She dithers endlessly.*

And this one. No, this one. No, this one.

**Mum** I'll find my purse, and see you out.

*Mum leaves the room. Mrs Harrison trails after her, busily unwrapping her chocolates. Gerald settles on the sofa, and Jude snuggles up beside him.*

**Jude**     (*wheedling*) Read to me, Gerald.

**Kitty**    (*imitating softly*) Read to me, Gerald. Pretty, pretty, please . . .

*Jude gives Kitty a glare. Gerald reaches over to unfold a paper lying on the arm of the sofa.*

**Gerald**   'Shares continued their steady revival today, with the FT Share Index finishing the week improving thirty-three point two points, to one thousand, seven hundred and fifty . . .

*Jude's thumb creeps into her mouth, and she snuggles closer.*

The FT 30 share index gained twenty-seven point three points to one thousand, four hundred and five, crossing the fourteen hundred points line for the first time in two months. Gilts improved by up to three quarters of a million – '

*Gerald breaks off suspiciously. He inspects the date on the top of the paper.*

Hang on! I thought that all sounded a bit familiar. This is yesterday's paper. Where's today's?

*Kitty moves forward quickly, but is too late. Gerald has reached for the paper on the table. When he picks it up, Kitty's essay slides onto the floor.*

Hello. What's this?

*Kitty bites her lip.*

**Kitty**    Nothing. Just a bit of rubbish. Don't bother with it. Just drop it in the bin.

*Gerald is about to crumple it up when he notices the writing on it.*

**Gerald**   No, I don't think so, Kitty. I think it's some of your homework.

**Kitty**    No, really! It's –

**Gerald**  No, listen.

*He holds it up and reads.*

'Something I hate comes round to our house practically every day now.

*Jude puts her head in her hands. Kitty hangs her head.*

Slimy and creepy and revolting, it makes me absolutely sick. It walks in here –

*Gerald stops. He gives Kitty a glance. Then he reads on, in a cooler tone.*

It walks in here and acts as if it owns the place. The first thing it does is switch off all the lights it thinks we don't need.

*He stops again, looking astonished. When he reads on, it is in a tone of sheer wonder.*

"There!" it says. "That should slow the little electric wheel down to a sprint!"'

*He stops, and looks around at all the lights that he switched off earlier. Then he lowers the sheet of paper and looks reproachfully at Kitty. Kitty stares back defiantly.*

**Jude**  (*bravely*) She didn't mean it, Gerald.

*Gerald is still looking at Kitty.*

**Gerald**  Oh, I think she did.

**Jude**  No, honestly. It was just a joke.

**Gerald**  A joke?

**Jude**  (*desperately*) Yes. A joke!

*Mum comes back in, closing her purse.*

**Mum**  A joke? Have I just missed a joke?

*There is a horrid silence. Then, suddenly, Gerald takes charge.*

**Gerald**  (*cheerfully*) That's right. You missed a joke.

**Mum**  What joke?

*Kitty and Jude look nervously at Gerald.*

| | |
|---|---|
| **Gerald** | All right. I'll tell it again. What did the cannibal with one leg say when they asked him if he enjoyed his holiday? |
| **Mum** | I don't know. What did he say? |
| **Gerald** | He said, 'It was excellent. Apart from the fact that it was self-catering.' |
| **Mum** | (*laughing*) Oh, that's horrible! |

*Mum turns to Kitty and Jude, who are staring at Gerald in disbelief.*

Don't you think it's funny?

*Gerald casually crumples up Kitty's essay.*

| | |
|---|---|
| **Gerald** | You can't expect them to laugh, Rosalind. They've already heard it. |

*He winks at Kitty, and drops the essay safely in the bin.*

| | |
|---|---|
| **Mum** | So. Anybody hungry? |
| **Gerald** | My turn to cook tonight, I think. Better get started. Do I have any willing helpers? |
| **Jude** | I'll help! |

*Gerald puts an arm round Jude.*

| | |
|---|---|
| **Gerald** | Good. We can get started on the homework, too. |

*Kitty steps forward.*

| | |
|---|---|
| **Kitty** | I'll – |

*Gerald stops and turns.*

| | |
|---|---|
| **Gerald** | Mmm? |
| **Kitty** | (*in a rush*) I'll help tonight, too. |
| **Jude** | (*delighted*) Kitty! |
| **Kitty** | (*embarrassed*) If you like. |

*Gerald raises an eyebrow at Kitty. Then he puts his other arm round her, and ushers them both to the kitchen.*

| | |
|---|---|
| **Gerald** | The more, the merrier. That's what I say. |

*Mum is left watching Kitty curiously as they walk away.*

**Mum**   (*softly, to herself*) Well, fancy that . . .


## Scene Four

*The living room.*

*Kitty is standing to the side. She speaks to the audience.*

**Kitty**   But it just wasn't that easy, I'm afraid. After Gerald Faulkner saved my bacon that day with Mum, I tried. I really did. After all, I could see that Jude was fond of him. And he did make Mum happy. So who was I to spoil things for everyone, just because I couldn't stand it? But I couldn't. The house didn't even seem like home to me any more, when he was there meddling in everything, goggling at Mum . . .

*The lights come up. Gerald is fixing a plug on one of the lamps. Mum walks in with an overflowing laundry basket. Gerald looks up.*

**Gerald**   That blouse completely changes the colour of your eyes, Rosalind. They've gone the most extraordinary blue.

*Kitty sticks a finger down her throat.*

**Kitty**   Op, plop! Pass the mop!

**Gerald**   And I love the way that skirt swings when you walk.

*Kitty walks into the scene.*

**Kitty**   Dad bought Mum that skirt.

**Mum**   (*astonished*) No, he didn't.

**Kitty**   Well, you used to wear it a lot when we were all together. You used to wear it when we visited Granny. But we don't see that Granny much any more. I miss her. I miss her a lot.

*Mum dumps the laundry basket on the table, hard. She starts to sort dried washing into piles.*

**Mum**      Mine. Kitty's. Jude's. These socks are mine, I think.

**Kitty**    You shrank them. Before that, they were Dad's.

**Mum**      Haven't you any more homework to finish, Kitty? Jude's. Kitty's. Mine.

**Kitty**    No, I've done it. I did it after I helped Jude with hers while you were out last night. Again.

**Mum**      For less than an hour.

**Kitty**    (*to Gerald*) Dad used to help her in the old days, of course. She misses Dad a lot.

**Mum**      What about your music practice? Have you done that?

**Kitty**    I did that after I phoned Dad.

**Mum**      Well, it's a nice weekend. Why don't you arrange something with one of your friends?

**Kitty**    (*pretending innocence*) Oh, I see! You want me to go! You want to be alone. I'm in your way.

*Picking up Flossie, she walks mournfully towards the door.*

(*in martyred tones*) Don't worry. I'll find something to do . . .

**Gerald**   If you're looking for something to do, Kitty, you could help your mother with the laundry. Why don't you carry your pile upstairs for her?

**Mum**      (*giggling*) And hang it neatly on your floor, as usual.

**Gerald**   Rosalind, the fact that Kitty's room is such a mess is not a joke. When I went in there half an hour ago to fix her radiator, I tripped over a pile of books on her floor, and she hadn't even bothered to open her curtains.

**Mum**      Don't tell me. I don't want to know.

**Gerald**   Honestly! It was a pit. Blackened banana skins. Shrivelled apple cores. Clothes all over, coated in cat hairs. Half-empty cups of stone-cold coffee, growing mould.

**Mum**   Take it easy, Gerald.

**Gerald**   No, honestly! Make-up spilling out on the dressing table. Pens leaking on the rug. Crumpled-up papers everywhere. Blouses and underwear fighting their way out of the drawers.

**Mum**   Designer compost!

**Gerald**   It isn't funny, Rosalind!

*Mum freezes.*

**Mum**   Oh, calm down, Gerald. Maybe you've just forgotten what kids Kitty's age are like.

*Gerald is hot under the collar now.*

**Gerald**   Don't try to tell me they all have floors thick with tangled electrical wires, and filthy dishes, and books in great untidy heaps!

*Mum winks at Kitty.*

**Mum**   I call it her open-plan filing system.

**Gerald**   And I call it *disgusting*. You're doing yourself no favours, letting your girls get away with murder.

**Mum**   Murder? Don't be ridiculous, Gerald!

**Gerald**   I mean it, Rosalind.

**Mum**   (*icily*) So do I, Gerald. For heaven's sake! Murder, indeed! Look at the planet we live on! Wars. Famine. Poverty. Pollution. My Kitty spends her time going to meetings, and shaking collecting cans under people's noses, and trying to improve things a bit for helpless animals. My Kitty goes round trying to explain to people that for the cost of one single sophisticated weapons system, we could afford a decent health service. What does it *matter* if her bedroom floor is knee-deep in knickers?

**Gerald**   All I'm saying is that you could do with a bit of help round here. You go to meetings, too. You rattle cans. And you have a full-time job. But you still manage to find a bit of time to clean up the bathroom after you, and mop the odd floor. And there's no reason on earth why Kitty shouldn't, either.

*Mum looks a bit taken aback.*

**Mum**    Well, maybe you've got a point there . . .

*Kitty gives her mother a furious look. Mum sees, and draws in her breath sharply.*

Ooh, Gerald. Maybe you should mind what you say. You're getting in terrible trouble with Kitty.

**Gerald**    I'm not afraid of Kitty. And I'll prove it.

*He picks up her pile of laundry and dumps it in her arms.*

Here you are. Another forkful for your compost heap.

*Kitty stands stock-still, giving him the evil eye. Gerald doesn't notice because he's turned away to pick up the desk lamp he's rewiring.*

I'm going to have to find a longer flex for this.

*Gerald goes out. Kitty is still standing stock-still.*

**Mum**    Well. Off you go.

**Kitty**    Not till you tell me.

**Mum**    (*baffled*) Not till I tell you what?

**Kitty**    To take this laundry upstairs. I'm not doing it till you tell me to do it.

**Mum**    But, Kitty. Gerald just told you.

**Kitty**    Yes. Gerald told me. And that's just the point. I won't take orders from Gerald. He's not my Dad.

*Mum prises the pile of laundry out of her hands.*

**Mum**    Oh, Kitty.

*Mum pulls Kitty to the sofa, and makes her sit down at her side. She pats her knee.*

I know he's not your Dad, Kitty. But it wasn't really 'an order', either. He was just saying what he thought.

**Kitty**    Well, he's no *business* to say what he thinks. He's nothing to do with us.

**Mum**  (*reprovingly*) Yes, he is, Kitty. He is, at the very least, a guest of mine.

*Kitty leaps to her feet.*

**Kitty**  Guest? Guest? He's not a guest. Guests don't behave like he does. Guests don't swan into other people's homes and tell their children what to do. Guests stay where you've put them, and do whatever you've suggested they do, till you suggest something else. Guests don't sprawl on the sofa reading the stock market reports until they get bored, then just get up and root through other people's cupboards, looking for spanners and wrenches. And guests don't wander into people's private bedrooms, searching for airlocks in the pipes!

**Mum**  Kitty! Who was it who complained the whole house was freezing? It was you! You came down this morning saying your bedroom had turned into the Arctic.

**Kitty**  (*sullenly*) That's not the point. I don't care if my carpet turns to permafrost. I don't want that man in there, nosing about.

**Mum**  Gerald wasn't 'nosing about'. He was very kindly fixing a problem in the heating system for me. And for you.

**Kitty**  (*bitterly*) If he wasn't nosing about, then why did he come straight downstairs and start criticizing everything he saw?

**Mum**  I'm not sure that's the fairest way of explaining what happened.

**Kitty**  I think it's perfectly fair. After all, that's what he's best at, isn't it? Criticizing everything I do.

**Mum**  Don't exaggerate, Kitty. Gerald doesn't criticize everything you do. He simply says what he thinks.

**Kitty**  And does what he likes! And comes and goes as he pleases! He's really dug himself in now, hasn't he, Mum? It's all, 'Kitty, will you just this?' and 'Kitty, could you just that?'

**Mum**   If the four of us are all in the house together –

**Kitty**  (*interrupting*) Exactly! But that's what you don't
          understand. That's what I'm trying to tell you –

          *Gerald appears in the doorway, holding the lamp.*
          *Nobody notices him.*

          We're all in the house together, but I don't want him
          here! He might be your friend, but he isn't mine!

          *Gerald backs out, closing the door silently.*

          And he can't tell me how to be, or what to do!
          Because he's not my Dad! And it is none of his
          business!

          *Mum sinks back down on the sofa.*

**Mum**   Oh, dear.

          *She sighs heavily.*

          I wish –

          *She breaks off, shaking her head.*

**Kitty**  What?

**Mum**   It doesn't matter.

**Kitty**  (*bitterly*) Too true. Wishing won't do you any good at
          all. Don't think I haven't tried wishing. It doesn't
          work.

          *Mum sinks her head in her hands.*

**Kitty**  Now what's the matter?

**Mum**   I don't know what to do, that's what's the matter!

**Kitty**  But I'm *telling* you what to do. That is exactly what
          I'm doing. I'm trying to explain that, if you want me to
          do things around the house, *you* have to ask me. I
          think that's perfectly reasonable. Don't leave it to
          *him*. Just say to me, 'Kitty, will you take your laundry
          upstairs?' And then I'll do it.

          *Mum looks up.*

**Mum**   Really?

**Kitty**  Really.

**Mum**   That simple?

**Kitty**   That simple.

**Mum**   All right. You win. We'll give it a little whirl.

*She stands up, faces Kitty, and clears her throat.*

Kitty, will you please carry your laundry up to your room?

**Kitty**   (*formally*) Yes, Mum. I'd be delighted.

*Kitty turns to go.*

**Mum**   Oh, and take Jude's with you, will you?

*Mum piles Jude's laundry on top. Kitty's smile becomes a little forced.*

**Kitty**   Okay, Mum.

**Mum**   (*relaxing into simple lack of tact*) Oh, and since you're going up there, can you drop mine off in my room as well?

*Mum heaps a further pile on Kitty, who is now hidden behind laundry.*

**Kitty**   (*in clipped tones*) Yours as well. Right.

*Kitty makes unsteadily for the door.*

**Mum**   Oh, and when you've done that, would you be an absolute poppet and dig me up a few of your potatoes?

*Kitty stops in her tracks.*
*Mum's hand shoots up to her mouth as she realizes just how much she's pushed her luck. She watches Kitty nervously. But with an obvious effort, Kitty carries on, still grimly smiling, out of the room.*

**Mum**   (*softly, to herself*) Steady on, Rosalind.

*Gerald pokes his head round the door. When he sees Kitty has gone, he comes in.*

**Gerald**   Is everything OK?

*Mum turns and stares at him. She takes a deep breath.*

**Mum**   (*bravely*) Oh, yes. No problems. None at all.

**Gerald**   (*gently*) I believe you. Thousands wouldn't.

| Mum | No, everything's fine. Honestly. It'll all work out. |
| Gerald | Rosalind . . . |

*He shakes his head sadly at her. Then he puts his arm around her and they walk out.*

## Scene Five

*Jude's bedroom.*

*It is remarkably tidy, with all her stuffed animals set in rows, all the books neatly shelved, and the toys in their baskets. A week's 'Financial Times' are stacked on her bedside table. Jude is kneeling on the floor, with scissors and sticky tape. She is covering her new homework exercise book with bright wrapping paper.*

*Kitty kicks open the door and strides in.*

| Kitty | Laundry! |

*She tosses Jude's clothes onto the bed so carelessly that they scatter.*

| Jude | Kitt-ee! |
| Kitty | Whoops. Sorry. |

*She gathers the clothes back in a pile.*

I always forget how horribly neat and tidy you keep your room. Goggle-eyes must love it in here.

| Jude | (*reproachfully*) Kitt-ee! |
| Kitty | What? |
| Jude | Don't call him that. |
| Kitty | What? |
| Jude | You know. |
| Kitty | Goggle-eyes? |
| Jude | Don't say it, Kitty. |
| Kitty | I can call him what I want. |

**Jude**     It's my room. And I don't like you calling him that in here.

**Kitty**    All right, then. Gerald.

*She makes a face.*

Gerald, Gerald, Gerald. He must love it in here. All clean and orderly. Everything in its place.

*She makes a performance of pushing one of the books a millimetre back in line on the shelf.*

Nothing and nobody sticking out like a sore thumb and causing any trouble.

**Jude**     You used to keep your bedroom tidy too.

**Kitty**    Only because they made me.

**Jude**     I like mine tidy anyway.

*Kitty picks a stuffed pony out of the tidy line of soft toys and inspects its bald patches critically.*

**Kitty**    I can't imagine bothering to put things in neat rows when there are so many other things to do.

*Jude keeps up her end of the conversation while working on her new cover.*

**Jude**     That's what you used to say to Mum and Dad.

**Kitty**    Did I?

**Jude**     Every Saturday morning.

**Kitty**    I don't remember that.

**Jude**     I do. Just after breakfast there would always be a great long argument about your room.

**Kitty**    Really?

**Jude**     Mum would tell you you had to clear it up before you went out. You'd say it was your room, so it was your business. So Mum would say that, on that argument, all the money in her purse was hers. So it was her business whether or not she gave you your pocket money that week.

**Kitty**    I don't remember that.

| | |
|---|---|
| **Jude** | Then Dad would say it wasn't your room anyway. He said that while he and Mum were paying all the mortgage, they owned all the rooms. And yours was a squalid and disgusting pit and a positive health hazard. |
| **Kitty** | Did he say that? |
| **Jude** | Yes, he did. And then he used to say you'd better get up there pretty sharpish and clean it up before he turned you over and paddled your bum. |
| **Kitty** | Oh, yes. It's all coming back now . . . |
| **Jude** | Then you'd always lose your temper, and scream and shout, and call him a horrible Adolf Hitler. |
| **Kitty** | That's right! |
| **Jude** | And he'd say – |

*Triumphantly remembering, Kitty interrupts with an imitation of her father.*

| | |
|---|---|
| **Kitty** | 'I should watch it if I were you, young lady. You're getting a little bit too big for your boots!' |
| **Jude** | Then you'd burst into tears and rush to Mum. And she would pat you on the back and tell you he wasn't really cross. And then we'd all have coffee. And then you used to go and clean your room. It used to take all morning. |
| **Kitty** | It's quite an awkward room to clean. |
| **Jude** | No, not to clean the room. To have the argument. |
| **Kitty** | Did it? All morning? |

*She looks thoughtful.*

Maybe that's why Mum doesn't bother any longer. Because it took all morning.

| | |
|---|---|
| **Jude** | Mum says she hasn't got the time or the energy any more. She says she's spent entire weeks of her life getting on at you about your room. She said to Mrs Harrison, 'Kitty only has to *glance* in a room for it to look as if a bomb just hit it.' |
| **Kitty** | Cheek! |

**Jude**  She says if she stayed on your case long enough and hard enough to keep you tidy all the time, she'd probably have to give up work.

**Kitty**  That's a bit of an exaggeration.

**Jude**  Mum says keeping you tidy is a Two-Man-Job.

**Kitty**  (*thoughtfully*) A Two-Man-Job? Does she really say that?

**Jude**  Quite often, yes.

*Jude holds up her finished cover.*

There! What do you think of that?

**Kitty**  Excellent. It looks really nice. But it's only a homework book. Why did you want to make it look so snazzy?

**Jude**  Because I'm moving up a set.

**Kitty**  I didn't know.

**Jude**  It's supposed to be a secret. But Mrs Fairbrother says that if I carry on the way I've been going –

**Kitty**  You mean with Gerald explaining it all to you every night?

**Jude**  That's right. If we keep on like that, I can go up a set. Mrs Fairbrother says she thinks I've finally got it sorted out.

**Kitty**  (*gently*) That's nice, Jude. I really hope it happens soon.

*Thoughtfully, Kitty bites her lip and turns to stare out of the window.*

**Jude**  (*confidently*) It will.

*Jude pauses and looks anxious.*

If Gerald stays . . .

**Kitty**  (*slowly*) If Gerald stays . . .

*Kitty turns back into the room. She paces restlessly while Jude gathers scraps of torn paper from the floor. On one of her circuits of the room, Kitty lifts a 'Financial Times' from beside the bed, stares at it, then drops it before asking her sister thoughtfully –*

You don't *mind*, do you?

**Jude**   Don't mind what?

**Kitty**   All of the things he thinks. That whether your stocks and shares go up or down is more important than animals stuffed in small cages, and people being bombed, and meadows being turned into car parks.

**Jude**   (*cautiously*) He's always very nice to me . . .

*Kitty reverses and paces the other way.*

**Kitty**   And Mum doesn't seem to mind that he's a political Neanderthal whose only serious worry is what blouse she wears . . .

**Jude**   He's very nice to her, as well.

**Kitty**   But what about *me*?

**Jude**   He always tries to be nice to you.

**Kitty**   He saved my bacon once. I'll give him that.

**Jude**   Twice.

**Kitty**   Really? How?

**Jude**   He found those scissors you swore to Mum you hadn't borrowed, up in your room.

*Kitty draws in her breath sharply.*

**Kitty**   I forgot to put them back!

**Jude**   And Mum was storming round the house, saying 'I *know* Kitty's taken them. I bet a million pounds they're somewhere in that stinking pit of hers.'

**Kitty**   What did he do?

**Jude**   He smuggled them into the toolbox. And left it open on the table. Then, next time Mum walked past, she noticed them, and snatched them up. 'I ought to kick myself,' she said. 'I'm going senile.'

**Kitty**   And what did *he* say?

**Jude**   Nothing.

**Kitty**   Nothing at all?

**Jude**   He went like this to me.

*She puts a warning finger on her lips.*

**Kitty**  He just let Mum think she'd put them there herself . . .
*Jude nods.*
You're right, then. That's twice. He's rescued me twice.

**Jude**  (*ruefully*) He rescues me every single morning with Mrs Fairbrother!

**Kitty**  All right. Fair's fair. I'll try again. He tries, so I'll try, too. I can't bring myself to *like* him. But I can try and get on with him a bit better. For you. And Mum.
*She hesitates.*
Yes. I can do it. I can definitely do it. As soon as I've dug up the potatoes, I'll go and be nice to Goggle-eyes. Sorry! Gerald. I'll go and be nice to Gerald. I'll manage it. I'll treat it like any other little job.
*She hesitates one last time.*
Yes. I can do it. Watch me. Off I go.
*Jude watches Kitty walk determinedly to the door and leave. When the door closes, Jude reaches down for the stuffed pony Kitty was stroking earlier.*

**Jude**  What do you reckon, Pony? Do you think it's going to be that easy?
*She pretends the soft toy is talking back to her.*
Neigh . . . Neigh . . .
*Jude sighs.*
Yes, Pony. That's what I think, too.


## Scene Six

*In the kitchen.*

*Mum and Gerald are preparing the lunch together. Gerald is in a pinny, slicing beans.*

**Gerald**  So I thought I'd put in for this Small Business of the Year award. After all, even though we've only been going a short time, I reckon we now take in at least

fifteen per cent of the printing work in this town.
Why, only last week –

*The door opens. Kitty comes in, hiding a bucket
behind her back.*

**Kitty** Hello.

**Mum** Hello, sweetheart.

**Gerald** Hello, Kitty.

**Kitty** Hello –

*Kitty makes a visible effort to say his name.*

– Gerald.

*Both Gerald and Mum look astonished. Mum's look
alters to one of slight suspicion.*

**Mum** What have you got hidden behind your back?

*Triumphantly, Kitty swings the bucket of very muddy
potatoes out in front of her.*

**Kitty** Ta-ra! Freshly dug potatoes!

*She dumps the bucket proudly on the table.*

**Mum** Oh, well done, Kitty!

**Kitty** Not at all.

**Gerald** There's nothing like home-grown potatoes.

*He picks a couple out, and inspects them.*

And these look brilliant. Some of the best I've ever
seen.

**Kitty** Thank you, Gerald.

*Mum looks delighted at this obvious truce.*

**Mum** You're a real poppet, Kits. I'll just rush up and fetch
my purse.

*Gerald looks puzzled.*

**Kitty** No, tell me where you left it, and I'll go and get it for
you.

**Mum** I think I left it by the telephone.

**Kitty** By the telephone. Right.

*Kitty goes out of the room.*

| | |
|---|---|
| **Gerald** | Why is she off for your purse, Rosalind? |
| **Mum** | So I can pay her for the spuds, of course. |
| **Gerald** | *Pay* her? |
| **Mum** | That's right. |

*Kitty comes back with the purse.*

| | |
|---|---|
| **Kitty** | There's about five kilos in there, I reckon. |

*Mum picks up the bucket.*

| | |
|---|---|
| **Mum** | Yes. That feels about right. So, let me see . . . |

*She dips in her purse.*

| | |
|---|---|
| **Gerald** | Just let me get this straight, will you? |

*He rests both hands on the table and leans across, like Prosecuting Counsel in a court.*

Kitty has just dug those potatoes out of the ground for you.

| | |
|---|---|
| **Mum** | Correct. |
| **Gerald** | And they're from the vegetable plot at the bottom of the garden. |
| **Mum** | The very same. |

*Mum tips the potatoes into the sink.*

| | |
|---|---|
| **Gerald** | Begun by her father, but now kept up by Kitty with a bit of help from Judith. |
| **Kitty** | (*bitterly*) Not *much* help. Jude spends most of her free time upside down on the swing. |
| **Gerald** | I think that's beside the point here. |
| **Mum** | Beside *what* point? |

*Kitty gives Gerald an impatient look.*

| | |
|---|---|
| **Kitty** | Beside *whose* point, I think you mean. |
| **Gerald** | No, please. Bear with me, both of you. This is important. I want to understand. I take it Rosalind buys all the seeds. |
| **Mum** | Right. |
| **Gerald** | And the gardening tools. |

| | |
|---|---|
| **Mum** | Everything. Trowels, beanpoles, fertilizers, netting, manure . . . |
| | *Gerald puts his hands on his hips and stares. He is obviously scandalized.* |
| **Gerald** | And Kitty *charges* you for the potatoes! |
| | *Kitty's mouth drops open.* |
| **Kitty** | So? What's wrong with that? |
| **Gerald** | What's wrong with that? I'll tell you what's wrong with it. It's simply appalling, that's what's wrong with it! |
| **Kitty** | I don't see why. |
| **Gerald** | Don't you? |
| **Kitty** | No, I don't. It's not as if I were a bagsnatcher, or something. In fact, I think it's perfectly fair. |
| **Gerald** | Perfectly fair? Why, it's truly disgusting! |
| | *Kitty abandons all attempts to stay polite.* |
| **Kitty** | Why? Why is it (*mocking him*) 'simply appalling' and 'truly disgusting'? I don't like gardening. Neither does Mum. It's a big chore. So now Dad's gone, Mum pays me for the vegetables, to keep me going. |
| **Gerald** | What about you? Have you paid her yet for the lunch she's cooking and the bath she cleaned? |
| **Mum** | But, Gerald. I'm her mother! |
| **Gerald** | You are her *family*. And she is yours. You shouldn't be paying for her co-operation. No one should have to bribe their close relations to pull their weight. The very idea is shameful. |
| **Mum** | (*thoughtfully*) Do you really think it is? |
| **Gerald** | Yes. Yes, I do. |
| **Mum** | You have to admit it works, though. Look how quickly Kitty got round to bringing me the potatoes. |
| **Gerald** | That is entirely beside the point. It is the principle of the thing. |
| **Mum** | Maybe you're right. I must say, I've never felt quite easy about it. I used to help my parents in the house, |

and they would never have dreamed of giving me money.

**Gerald**   I should think not. The whole idea is repellent.

*Outraged, Kitty is giving Gerald the evil eye.*

**Mum**   But, Gerald. It does seem fairer to pay Kitty something now Judith's big enough to do her share, yet never does.

**Gerald**   Rosalind, if you do anything, you should be fining Judith till she does fair shares, not handing out great bribes to Kitty.

**Kitty**   Great bribes! Great bribes! I'm hardly going to get rich on what Mum gives me for each bucketful!

**Gerald**   Oh, ho! Oh, ho! Be warned, all mothers everywhere! Already she's angling for a rise, our little potato entrepreneur!

**Mum**   (*giggling*) Oh, dear, Kitty! Looks like, if Gerald gets his way, you've had your chips!

*She doubles up with mock laughter.*

Geddit? Had your chips?

*Gerald covers his eyes, laughing and wincing.*

**Gerald**   Oh, Rosalind. What a terrible joke. That is the worst I've ever heard you make.

*He puts his arm round her and squeezes.*

**Mum**   (*laughing*) Oh, I make plenty worse than that. Don't I, Kitty?

*Kitty is silent and set-faced. She watches them, arm in arm, laughing together.*

Kitty?

*The silence lasts. Mum's tone changes.*

Kitty? Kitty?

*Mum drops Gerald's arm and rushes to take Kitty by both hands.*

Kitty, my love? Are you crying?

*Fiercely, Kitty shakes her head.*

You are! You're crying, sweetheart!

*Again, Kitty shakes her head, dashing tears from her cheeks. Her voice is choky.*

**Kitty**   No. No, I'm not.

**Mum**   Kitty! My precious!

*Kitty stands stock-still and unresponsive. Gerald hastily takes off his pinny.*

**Gerald**   I'll just nip out and get that tonic water. Before the shops shut on us.

*He picks up his jacket and hurries out, glancing back anxiously. The moment he disappears, Kitty collapses, weeping copiously.*

**Mum**   Kit-kats! What's the matter, sweetheart? What's wrong? Tell me, love. I can't do anything till you explain.

*She pulls Kitty down on her knee on a chair.*

**Kitty**   (*wailing*) I'm just fed up with him!

**Mum**   Gerald?

**Kitty**   Who else? I can't stand him! Always there! Always poking in! Always meddling! Even when I try, like I was doing just then, he ruins it. He wellies in, saying what he thinks all the time!

**Mum**   Oh, Kitty. He doesn't mean to –

**Kitty**   (*interrupting*) And what he thinks is never what we think! And I'm so sick of him!

**Mum**   Oh, Kitty, sweetheart!

*She pats Kitty on the back as if she were tiny.*

**Kitty**   And he's around all the time! He's here practically every day now. And things are different when he's around. Even you're different.

**Mum**   Me?

**Kitty**   Yes. You're different too.

**Mum**   How?

**Kitty**   I can't explain it. But you are. And being home isn't like it used to be when there were just the three of us. Or when we were with Dad.

**Mum**   (*comforting*) Oh, I know, sweetheart. I know.

**Kitty**   And I'm so fed up with him. He makes me feel so squashed. Can't we just have one quiet weekend without him? Can't we start now? Make some excuse to tell him to go home. You could say that I'm sickening for something. And we could have the weekend all to ourselves for once, just like before. Eating bananas squashed up in front of the telly. Can we? Can we, Mum? Please?

**Mum**   But, Kitty. Tomorrow is the big demonstration against the new car park.

**Kitty**   That's OK. We can just squash up three on a seat on the bus, as usual. And we'll be back before supper.

**Mum**   (*uneasily*) But, you see, I've invited Gerald to come along.

*Kitty springs to her feet.*

**Kitty**   Mu-um!

**Mum**   I'm sorry, Kitty.

**Kitty**   But why? Why did you do that? He doesn't believe in any of it. He doesn't care. He's already said he thinks the town doesn't have nearly enough car parking spaces. More customers for him is all he thinks about! So why is he tagging along? Just for the laugh?

**Mum**   I think he's curious. He sees us going off to all these meetings and things . . . I don't know. Anyhow, he asked if he could come along with us. And I said yes.

**Kitty**   (*eagerly*) Tell him you've changed your mind. Just tell him that.

*Mum gives this a moment's thought. Then –*

**Mum**   I can't do that. I'm sorry, love. I would if I could. But I can't. I don't mind telling him the truth – that *you'd* prefer it if he didn't come. But I can't tell him that I've changed *my* mind.

*Kitty rubs her eyes.*

**Kitty**   Don't tell him. If he has to come tomorrow, then he has to come. But you're not to tell him I mind. Promise me.

**Mum**   Honestly, Kitty. He is not a monster. He'd understand how you feel.

**Kitty**   No! I won't have Gerald Faulkner feeling sorry for me! And I won't have him knowing how much he upsets me!

**Mum**   Don't you think it would be easier if –

**Kitty**   Mum! I can't help the way I feel. I didn't *ask* for all this to happen round me! And if there's only one way I can deal with it, it's not my fault!

**Mum**   But it would be so much simpler to –

**Kitty**   Don't talk to me about 'simpler'! Everyone should have thought of that before! What you all so conveniently forget is that things are much simpler if it's your own Dad in the house!

*Mum is shocked. She bites her lip. Then she reaches out for Kitty again.*

**Mum**   Oh, Kitty. I'm so sorry things worked out this way.

*They hold each other close. Kitty is weeping again. Mum pats her back. She's very upset as well. Jude appears in the doorway, holding Pony. She whispers sadly in his ear.*

**Jude**   See, Pony? Not that easy. We were right.

*Gerald appears in the doorway behind Jude, holding a bottle of tonic. Over Jude's head, he looks anxiously at Rosalind and Kitty, who do not notice him. He slides an arm around Jude. She turns immediately towards him and buries herself against him for comfort.*

*End of Act One*

# ACT TWO

## Scene One

*In the living room.*

*Kitty is on the phone. At her feet is a large banner, wrapped between two poles.*

**Kitty**    What do you mean, 'What's wrong with him?' He's *horrible*, that's what's wrong with him . . . I'm *not* exaggerating, Dad. He's slimy and creepy and revolting. He makes me absolutely sick. I only have to *look* at him and I want to throw up . . . What *about* Jude? . . . Well, Jude sort of likes him, actually . . . (*sullenly*) No . . . No . . . (*through gritted teeth*) No, Dad. I don't think I *will* get used to him . . . No . . . No . . . Yes . . . All right . . . Yes . . . Goodbye.

*Kitty hangs up. She lifts Flossie from the sofa and cuddles her.*

## Scene Two

*Kitty addresses the audience.*

**Kitty**    See? Nobody listens. No one really cares. They're all too wrapped up in their own lives. And I feel terrible. How would you feel if you were totally outnumbered in your own home? It's horrible enough when you want something different from everybody around you. But when you know that, if you get your way, everyone else will feel dreadful, you feel even worse. Whose feelings are supposed to count for most? Mine? Mum's? Or Jude's?

*From offstage.*

**Jude**    Kitty! We're leaving now. Are you coming?

*Kitty puts Flossie back, picks up her rolled banner,
and walks unenthusiastically towards the door.*

**Kitty**   I'm coming, yes.


# Scene Three

*We are on the muddy edge of a new road-building
site. Along one side is a fence with a large sign: 'Keep
Out. Road Construction in Progress.' A motley group
of demonstrators is spilling off the hired bus with
banners, signs, sandwiches, wire-cutters, etc. Gerald
stands out in his smart suit.*

**Gerald**   My God! What a bus ride!

**Kitty**   (*sarcastically*) Don't worry, Mum. He probably hasn't
been on a bus for years. He's probably forgotten you
have to share a seat, and not everybody gets their
own window.

**Mum**   I'm sorry, Gerald. It must have really hurt when all
those banner poles fell on your head.

**Gerald**   It was actually the constant hymn-singing I found the
most painful aspect of the journey.

**Jude**   Those weren't hymns. Those were battle-songs.

**Gerald**   (*contemptuously*) 'Save all the pretty flowers, quick!
Save all the lovely trees!'

**Jude**   What's wrong with that?

**Gerald**   I wouldn't mind, but we've been on that bus nearly
two hours. Why couldn't it have left promptly at nine?

**Mum**   Because nobody but us had arrived by then.

**Gerald**   And why not?

**Mum**   It's not that easy to arrange these things. Some
people thought that it was nine o'clock. Others were
told that we were leaving at ten.

**Gerald**   It's not too taxing a notion to take on board, is it? 'We
start at nine.' The roadbuilders over there can
obviously manage it. So why can't your group?

| | |
|---|---|
| **Kitty** | (*tartly*) Because we don't have hundreds of thousands of pounds of taxpayers' money to keep our organization running like clockwork. And the roadbuilders do. |
| **Gerald** | And how come there are so few of you? |
| **Mum** | Because the fliers didn't get posted out in time. |
| **Gerald** | Why not? Fliers are simple enough to print and send. My firm shifts thousands of them every day. |
| **Kitty** | For people who have enough money to pay you. |

*A middle-aged woman in flowery clothes comes up to offer home-made biscuits out of a plastic carton.*

| | |
|---|---|
| **Beth** | Have one of my wholemeal crackers, Rosie. |
| **Mum** | Thanks, Beth. Did you meet Gerald on the bus? |
| **Beth** | Hello, Gerald. I saw you on the bus. But from the way you were dressed, I assumed you must be a police nark. I warn you, you're likely to get that suit filthy. |

*Gerald looks down at his clothing.*

| | |
|---|---|
| **Gerald** | Why? Holding the demo in a pigsty, are we? |
| **Mum** | Sssh! Gerald! |
| **Beth** | Would you like one of my home-made crackers? |

*Gerald fastidiously prises one apart from its fellows.*

| | |
|---|---|
| **Gerald** | Ah, wheatgerm petits fours. How very – |

*He chews with difficulty.*

| | |
|---|---|
| | – unusual. |
| **Beth** | Kitty? Want one? |
| **Kitty** | Ta, Beth. |

*She takes a cracker. Beth leads her to one side.*

| | |
|---|---|
| **Beth** | Kitty, who is that man beside your mother? He's not Rosie's new boyfriend, is he? |
| **Kitty** | Good heavens, no! He's – He's a cousin of hers! Over from Perth. |
| **Beth** | Well, I suppose you pick your friends. But no one can be blamed for their flesh and blood. How long is he staying with you? |

| **Kitty** | Too long. Mum's very patient, though. |
| **Beth** | Too patient, I reckon. |
| | *Beth glares at Gerald's back before moving away.* |
| **Gerald** | The bus driver's got some sense, anyhow. He's slipping away for a quiet read of the papers. |
| **Kitty** | Why don't you push off with him? |
| **Gerald** | Excuse me? |
| **Mum** | (*hastily*) What Kitty means, Gerald, is wouldn't you be happier sitting on the bus with him? You could put your feet up and read the papers as well. |
| **Gerald** | But I want to be here with you. |
| **Kitty** | But why? |
| **Gerald** | Well, for the pleasure of your company, of course. |
| **Kitty** | But you have the pleasure of our company practically every day. It's mad to want an extra few hours of it. |
| **Gerald** | I don't see why. Surely wanting an extra few hours of your company is no madder than wanting your company at all. |
| | *Kitty looks thoroughly confused. Gerald turns round in a circle on the spot, assessing the site.* |
| | What a mess! |
| | *He points offstage.* |
| | Look, Rosalind! Three more vans stopping just across the track of mud. That'll make a few more of you. |
| **Mum** | Don't be so silly, Gerald. That's the police. |
| **Gerald** | Police? How come they're here before you even start? |
| **Kitty** | They always arrive first. They're always more efficient than we are. If we're supposed to be here at ten o'clock, they're here at ten o'clock. Even if we don't turn up till eleven. |
| **Gerald** | Don't you keep your plans secret? |
| **Mum** | Why should we keep our plans secret? Acres of precious countryside are torn up every day. If we |

didn't tell reporters and television and radio and everybody who'll listen where we are, we'd find ourselves demonstrating against one bored bloke in a bulldozer who wants to get home for his tea.

*Mum turns to Beth and the others.*

What do we think? Time to get moving?

**Beth**    Righty-ho.

*The demonstrators hold up their placards and unfurl their banners. Kitty is struggling with hers. Gerald steps forward and prises one of the poles out of her hand.*

**Gerald**    Kitty, let me help you with that.

**Kitty**    I'm all right.

**Gerald**    Don't be silly. Let me help.

*He steps back to look at it. One corner of it is clear white, with one small dot inside. The whole of the rest of the banner is covered in dots, like measles run riot.*

So what's all this, then?

**Kitty**    Do you really want to know?

**Gerald**    Yes. Yes, I do. If I'm going to carry one end of it, I'd like to know what it's about.

*Kitty points to the rash of dots all over the banner.*

**Kitty**    Well, every one of these dots represents a million pounds spent on firepower.

**Gerald**    Firepower?

**Kitty**    You know. Bombs. Nuclear weapons. Mines.

**Gerald**    Oh, right.

*Kitty points to the lonely little dot in the corner.*

**Kitty**    And this dot here represents the amount spent on conservation.

**Gerald**    In the same time?

**Kitty**    In the same time.

*Gerald whistles through his teeth.*

**Gerald**   My golly! It makes me quite dizzy, looking at all those dots. Firepower, eh?

**Kitty**    That's right. Anything that kills and maims and blackens and burns and poisons and ruins.

**Gerald**   (*thoughtfully*) And this little dot in the corner . . .

**Kitty**    Planting, saving, rescuing.

**Gerald**   The poor old planet. It makes you think . . .

*Kitty lifts her end of the banner and moves off.*

**Kitty**    (*softly*) I hope so!

*Gerald picks up his end and follows.*

**Gerald**   Who would have thought it? All those dots . . .

*They join the others, standing by the wire fence.*

**Beth**     Right. Time to get started. Who's snowballing today?

**Gerald**   (*softly to Kitty and Jude*) Snowballing? In this weather? What is the woman on about? Is she unhinged?

*Kitty rolls her eyes.*

**Jude**     Not *snowballing*, Gerald. *Snowballing*.

**Gerald**   It remains a mystery to me how one can throw snowballs when there is no snow.

**Kitty**    It isn't that sort of snowball. Groups like us are doing this all over the country. Two people get over the fence and stop the diggers. So the police arrest them. Next time, we make sure there are four. Then eight. And then sixteen. Then thirty-two. Then sixty-four. Then –

*Kitty stops, struggling with the maths.*

**Gerald**   One hundred and twenty-eight.

**Kitty**    Thank you. Except we haven't got that far. Today we're still on eight.

**Gerald**   But what's the point?

**Beth**     What do you mean, what's the point?

**Gerald**   I mean, why do you bother?

| | |
|---|---|
| **Mum** | Why do we bother doing anything? Because it's important. We do it for the same reason we march, and sit up trees people are trying to cut down, and write our letters to the newspapers, and nag our politicians. We do it all because we *care*. |
| **Gerald** | But what's the point of getting yourselves arrested? |
| **Mum** | Listen, Gerald. There are millions of people who think the way we do. Millions. People of all sorts. If we get ourselves arrested, then people get to know. We get to speak in court. People read about us in the newspapers. So gradually they get to see we're not just layabouts and ne'er-do-wells. We're not all nutcases, or people with nothing better to do. A lot of us have jobs and homes and families, just like them. And we object to what is going on in all our names. |
| **Gerald** | All very well. But then what? |
| **Beth** | You pay the fine. Or you refuse, because you can't. Or won't. |
| **Gerald** | And then you go to jail! |
| **Mum** | Better than going to the lions. And people have done that before now for their beliefs. |
| **Beth** | We're never going to go anywhere at this rate. Come on, everybody. Let's get started, for heaven's sake. Unfurl your banners. Hold up your signs. Off we go! |

*Kitty raises one end of her banner.*

| | |
|---|---|
| **Kitty** | Jude, hold the other end. |
| **Jude** | Oh, Kitty, no. It's too heavy for me. |
| **Kitty** | Don't act the baby, Jude. |
| **Jude** | Honestly, Kits. It makes my arms ache. |
| **Kitty** | You never do anything to help. |
| **Jude** | I do! |
| **Kitty** | No, you don't. You never help in the garden. You never do the washing up. You always wriggle out of everything. |
| **Jude** | I don't! |

| | |
|---|---|
| **Kitty** | You do! |
| **Gerald** | Why don't I hold it for now, and you two can argue later. Will that be OK? |
| **Kitty** | OK. |

*She adds, a little unwillingly –*

Thanks.

*Jude slinks away, to stand beside her mother. Beth gathers the snowballers in a line. They include a nun, an elderly lady and a middle-aged man.*

| | |
|---|---|
| **Beth** | Right. Let's have a look at today's heroes and heroines. One. Two. Three. And you again, Sister Marie-Claire. You're a brick! |

*Jude starts to drag on Mum's arm.*

| | |
|---|---|
| **Jude** | I'm hungry, Mum. |
| **Mum** | For heaven's sake, Jude. We haven't even started yet. |
| **Jude** | I'm still hungry. |
| **Mum** | You should have eaten more breakfast. |

*Beth has turned to the elderly lady now.*

| | |
|---|---|
| **Beth** | Five. Are you sure you're up to it this time, Mrs Hurley? You're looking quite peaky. |
| **Gerald** | (*to Kitty*) Someone of her age shouldn't be out here in this wind. |
| **Kitty** | She used to fly her kite up here when she was young. That's why she wants to save it. |
| **Beth** | Six. How are you, Dr Helstrom? You look nice and warm. Who's seven? Oh, that's me, of course. So who is missing? Who is number eight? |
| **Mrs Hurley** | Ben's number eight today. |
| **Beth** | I saw him on the bus. Where has he gone? |

*Ben rushes up, zipping his flies.*

| | |
|---|---|
| **Ben** | Sorry. |
| **Beth** | Eight. Right. Ready to go? |
| **Jude** | I'm really hungry. Can't I have a sandwich now? |
| **Mum** | Not now, Jude. |

**Jude**   (*whining*) And I'm cold. When are we going home?

**Mum**   Please don't start whining, Jude. You know I can't stand it.

*Jude makes a face and moves closer to Gerald. The demonstrators are moving off.*

**Gerald**   Go easy, Rosalind. It's been a tiring morning.

**Mum**   For heaven's sake, Gerald! It hasn't been that tiring. When I was young, we had to get up this early every single Sunday, to sit for over an hour in a stone-cold church, bored stiff. And that was just to save our own selfish little souls. Jude's lucky. A few weekends a year she gets a couple of hours' fresh air to save the whole world's bacon. Is that so terrible?

*Mum storms off, taking Jude with her, after the others.*

**Gerald**   Ouch!

**Kitty**   Don't mind her. She doesn't mean to get so ratty. It's just she hates spending her one day off a week dragging round muddy road sites and sitting down in front of bulldozers. She just wishes things would change, so she can stay home.

**Gerald**   I expect the police over there wish she'd stay home as well.

**Kitty**   Don't let her hear you saying that. Mum says at least it's their job to pitch out. They're paid to do it.

**Gerald**   I'm sure they have plenty of other useful things to do.

**Kitty**   And so has Mum! She has a lot more things to do than any of them. She has a full-time job, just like they do. And then, on top of that, she has a house to run and Jude and me to care for. You'd better not let her hear you saying *she's* wasting *their* time. She'll be a whole lot more bothered about wasting her own!

*Gerald raises his end of the banner.*

**Gerald**   Time to move nearer. I see the officers are closing in.

**Kitty**   Mum's not afraid of the police.

**Gerald**   No need to ask for trouble.

*Gerald and Kitty catch up with the others. The police officers come across to the snowballers.*

**Beth**   Right! Through the fence we go.

**Police Officer 1**   (*warningly*) Criminal trespass.

**Beth**   Sunday afternoon down at the station, here we come.

**Police Officer 2**   And Monday morning, too, unless you're lucky.

**Gerald**   (*to Kitty*) Is that officer trying to threaten your mother? If she is, her superintendent's certainly going to hear about it from me.

**Kitty**   Why? What would you do?

**Gerald**   I'd write a letter of complaint, of course.

**Kitty**   Really?

**Gerald**   I've done it before, and I can do it again.

**Kitty**   When? When have you done it before?

**Gerald**   I'll tell you later. Ssh! I'm listening.

**Ben**   What does she mean: 'And Monday morning, too'?

*Beth lowers her wire cutters.*

**Beth**   I don't know.

*To the officer.*

What do you mean?

**Police Officer 1**   We're very short-staffed this weekend. And, as I understand it, there are eight of you. Twice as many as last time. That's quite a bit of paperwork. She's right. There's always the risk that some of it might not get finished today.

**Beth**   Oh, well. I suppose, if something's important enough –

**Ben**   Hang on, Beth! I have a problem here! I can't risk being held overnight. I have an exam at nine o'clock tomorrow.

**Beth**   But, Ben. You're our number eight!

**Mum**   Beth! Be reasonable! The poor lad has an exam. You have to let him off.

**Beth**   But we need eight. What sort of group is it that can't even manage to find eight people for a snowball?

| | |
|---|---|
| **Gerald** | (*softly*) Same sort of group as can't get a bus to leave by nine. |
| | *Mum overhears, and spins round angrily.* |
| **Mum** | What did you say? |
| **Gerald** | I said, 'The same sort of – ' |
| **Mum** | No! Don't repeat it, since it isn't true! And I'll prove it's not true, Gerald. |
| | *Mum turns to Beth.* |
| **Mum** | Here you are, Beth. We do have eight for the snowball after all. |
| **Beth** | Who's doing it? |
| **Mum** | I am. |
| **Kitty** | Mum! No! |
| **Jude** | Mu-um! |
| **Gerald** | Rosalind! I can't believe I'm hearing this! |
| **Mum** | Don't worry, Kitty. Jude, it'll be fine. Mrs Harrison will come round and sit for you. |
| **Kitty** | But you might be away all night! |
| **Gerald** | Rosalind, for heaven's sake, be sensible! |
| **Mum** | Don't try and tell me what's sensible for my own family, Gerald. There's nothing sensible about sitting back quietly and being no trouble while a few rich and selfish people chew up the planet your children have to live on! There's nothing sensible about always being there to look after them now, if their future is going to be ruined. There's nothing – |
| **Beth** | Rosie! Are you standing for political office? Or are you coming with us? |
| **Mum** | I'm coming with you. |
| **Jude** | Oh, Mu-um! Don't go! |
| **Mum** | Now listen, Kits. Make sure you phone Mrs Harrison the minute you get back. And there's a pizza in the freezer. Don't forget to pre-heat the oven, and – |
| **Kitty** | I know how to heat up a pizza, Mum! |

| | |
|---|---|
| **Mum** | Well, don't forget to – |
| **Beth** | Rosie! This is no time to spoon out cookery hints. Now come along! |

*Beth drags Mum off towards the others. Mum leans back.*

| | |
|---|---|
| **Mum** | (*wistfully*) Bye! |
| **Kitty** | (*anxiously*) Bye! |
| **Jude** | (*in a tearful whisper*) Bye! |
| **Mum** | Take care, now! |

*Beth drags Mum out of sight. Gerald stares after them.*

| | |
|---|---|
| **Gerald** | (*scornfully*) Pizza! |
| **Kitty** | What's wrong with pizza? |
| **Gerald** | What's wrong with it? After a strenuous day like this? One pokey frozen pizza between three of us? |
| **Jude** | Are you going to stay? |
| **Gerald** | Of course I'm going to stay. Somebody has to act responsibly, after all. I'll stay and eat with you, and then I'll stay and look after you. |
| **Jude** | Till Mum gets back? |
| **Gerald** | I wouldn't dream of leaving until she's safely through the door. |

*Jude slides her hand in Gerald's.*

| | |
|---|---|
| **Jude** | Goody! |
| **Kitty** | So I won't have to phone Mrs Harrison? |
| **Gerald** | No, you won't have to phone Mrs Harrison. I shall be there. |
| **Jude** | Goody! |

*He leads Jude towards the bus. Kitty runs after him and tugs at his sleeve.*

| | |
|---|---|
| **Kitty** | Gerald – |

*Gerald drops Jude's hand, and turns.*

| | |
|---|---|
| **Gerald** | Kitty? |
| **Kitty** | Gerald, will Mum be all right? |

| Gerald | Of course she will. It's all very tiresome, but she'll be perfectly, perfectly safe, I promise you. |
|---|---|
| Kitty | Really? |
| Gerald | Really. I mean that, Kitty. She'll be fine. |

*Kitty turns away. Gerald takes her gently by the shoulders and turns her back to face him. He takes a handkerchief from his pocket and wipes the tears on her cheeks.*

| Gerald | Do you believe me, Kitty? |
|---|---|

*Kitty nods unconvincingly.*

| Gerald | No, say it, Kitty. |
|---|---|

*There's a long silence. Then –*

| Kitty | Yes. I believe you. |
|---|---|

*Kitty has surprised herself. She cheers up.*

Yes! Yes, I do! I believe you!

| Gerald | Come on then, girls. Let's go and kick-start that bus driver into rounding everyone up, and getting us all home before we grow beards down to our feet. |
|---|---|
| Kitty | Righty-ho! |
| Jude | Girls don't grow beards! |
| Kitty | What about my banner? |
| Gerald | I'd rather hoped that you'd forgotten that. |
| Kitty | (*reproachfully*) Gerald! |
| Gerald | Oh, all right. Come on. Take an end. |

*Together they roll it up, and stride off. Gerald keeps one protective arm round Kitty. Jude bounds off cheerfully ahead.*

## Scene Four

*The empty living room.*

*The phone rings. Kitty bursts from the kitchen. She is wearing an apron and she dangles spaghetti from a fork. She calls back over her shoulder –*

**Kitty**   And, Gerald! Don't let Jude eat all my grated cheese!

*She lifts the phone.*

(*eagerly*) Mum? . . . (*astonished*) Oh, Mrs Harrison! How did you know – ? . . . No, Mrs Harrison. Mum must have been ringing from the police station, not the bus station . . . No, honestly. We're fine. Gerald is staying with us. . . . Yes, all night if he has to. . . . Yes, he is cooking something sensible and nourishing. . . . Yes. Perfectly safe, I promise you. . . . Yes, Mrs Harrison. Perfectly safe. . . . Bye!

*She puts down the phone, throws back her head like a fire-eater, twirls the spaghetti off the fork and down her throat.*

Yum!

## Scene Five

*The kitchen.*

*Jude and Gerald both wear aprons too. Jude is sloppily slicing tomatoes.*

**Gerald**   Come on, now. Do it properly. Thinner than that.

*Jude looks ready to argue. Then meekly she lowers her head and slices more carefully. Kitty picks up her grater and carries on with the cheese.*

**Kitty**   Can we stay up in case Mum gets back tonight?

| | |
|---|---|
| **Gerald** | You can. Judith can't. |
| **Jude** | Why can't I? |
| **Gerald** | Because you're younger, that's why. |
| **Jude** | That doesn't make any difference. |
| **Gerald** | It does if I say so. |
| **Jude** | Mum never says things like that. |
| **Gerald** | Perhaps she'd find this house ran better if she did. |

*Jude makes a face. Gerald puts a cocktail glass down beside the tomatoes.*

| | |
|---|---|
| **Jude** | Smashing! Fizz, lemon, ice-cubes! Mum never makes us drinks like this! |
| **Gerald** | Too busy arguing with you about your bedtime. |

*He hands a glass to Kitty.*

| | |
|---|---|
| **Kitty** | Oh, ta! Lovely. |

*Gerald raises his own glass.*

| | |
|---|---|
| **Gerald** | Cheers! |

*Kitty raises hers.*

| | |
|---|---|
| **Kitty** | Cheers! |

*She inspects it.*

They are cheery, aren't they? This glass is actually sparkling.

| | |
|---|---|
| **Gerald** | That's because I polished it. |
| **Kitty** | Polished it? |
| **Gerald** | On a tea towel. |

*He catches her look of mystification.*

There's quite a lot you two still have to learn about natty housekeeping, isn't there? Now. Is the table set properly?

*With a look of stern distaste, he lifts Flossie off the table and drops her on the floor.*

Right. And Rosalind's share is warming safely in the oven. So off we go.

*He dishes up.*

Elbows off the table, Jude.

**Jude** Mum never minds.

**Gerald** I expect she's too frazzled to notice. But I do. And I mind.

*Jude shrugs and takes her elbows off the table.*

**Kitty** (*curiously*) You really care about what things look like, don't you, Gerald? Carefully sliced tomatoes. Neatly set tables. Tidy bedrooms . . .

**Gerald** Yes. Yes, I think I do.

**Kitty** But surely the way things look isn't all that important.

**Gerald** Maybe it's not. But it still counts. And it can make a difference. You take your friends in the group. Most of them go round looking like a pack of scruffpots –

**Kitty** Scruffpots!

**Gerald** You can't deny it. Some of them look as if they've hauled their demo gear out of a dustbin behind Oxfam.

**Kitty** What does it matter what we look like, for heaven's sake? It's what we do that counts.

*Gerald leans forward and points at Kitty with his fork.*

**Gerald** Not so! You take your mother, for example –

**Jude** (*sanctimoniously*) Don't point your fork at people, Gerald.

*Hastily, Gerald complies.*

**Kitty** What about Mum?

**Gerald** Your mother goes off to work at that hospital every morning looking thoroughly respectable. But does she wear her anti-road badge? No. So no one ever gets the chance to think: 'What a nice, helpful woman! And yet she's one of that group fighting the new road. They can't all be layabouts, as I'd been led to think.'

**Kitty** They only call us layabouts because it's much simpler to insult us than win against us in fair

|          |                                                                                                                                                                                                                                                                   |
|----------|-------------------------------------------------------------------------------------------------------------------------------------------------------------------------------------------------------------------------------------------------------------------|
|          | argument. What did they call the people who wanted to end slavery?                                                                                                                                                                                                 |
| Gerald   | I don't know. Meddlers? Troublemakers?                                                                                                                                                                                                                             |
| Kitty    | Right. And all the women who wanted to have the vote.                                                                                                                                                                                                              |
| Gerald   | Let me guess. Hoydens. Vandals. Disgraces to their sex!                                                                                                                                                                                                            |
| Kitty    | Mum says as soon as your opponents are reduced to insulting you personally, you know you're on the way to victory.                                                                                                                                                 |
| Gerald   | But you could get there so much quicker, Kitty! Look at the members in your group. Most of them lead sensible lives, after all. If they tried dressing like the professionals they are, it would be harder to dismiss them. They would be treated with a whole lot more respect. |
| Kitty    | (*giggling*) Could you be coming round to our side, Gerald? Spooning out all these handy hints!                                                                                                                                                                    |
| Gerald   | Not at all. It's just that, being a small businessman, I can't bear inefficiency. Wherever I see it, I want to root it out. That's why I got so irritable when you were singing all those silly hymns.                                                              |
| Jude     | Not hymns, Gerald. I told you. Battle songs.                                                                                                                                                                                                                       |
| Gerald   | Whatever. Those tuneless dirges, anyway. The time could have been much more usefully employed. You could have spent it far more profitably writing yet again to your MP and all the local newspapers.                                                               |
| Kitty    | 'Profitably.' 'Usefully employed.' That's how you think about things around you, isn't it, Gerald?                                                                                                                                                                 |
| Gerald   | I suppose it is.                                                                                                                                                                                                                                                   |
| Kitty    | But don't you find it a strange way of looking at this lovely green planet of ours?                                                                                                                                                                                |
| Gerald   | Strange?                                                                                                                                                                                                                                                           |
| Kitty    | Well – boring, really.                                                                                                                                                                                                                                             |
| Gerald   | Oh, boring! (*thoughtfully*) Well, no. I've always thought about things that way, I suppose.                                                                                                                                                                       |

| Kitty | But, Gerald. Suppose one day you woke up and looked round, and had a vision? |
|---|---|
| **Gerald** | A vision? |
| Kitty | Yes. Suppose you suddenly looked at the trees and clouds and birds and animals. Really looked. And saw. And realized that everyone only has a hundred years at most to live on the earth, and look round them, and be happy. If you suddenly saw the world the way we see it – all bright and shining and there for everyone, if they'll just take care of it – then wouldn't you stop thinking about things the way you do? |
| **Gerald** | Which way? |
| Kitty | You know. Saying things like 'more profitably' and 'usefully employed'. And reading the stock market reports out loud to Jude every night. |
| **Gerald** | You mean 'the boring way', don't you? |
| Kitty | I suppose I do. |
| **Gerald** | You know, Kitty, sometimes I do think I might be boring. Today I watched you and your mother fighting to save a few yards of grass and a few trees, and I thought, 'No, I've never felt that strongly. Even when I was young.' So maybe I'm too blind to see what you see. Too numb to feel what you feel. But I can't help it. I was born that way. |

*Jude pats Gerald's hand comfortingly.*

| **Jude** | Poor Gerald! |
|---|---|
| Kitty | And doesn't it bother you? |
| **Gerald** | No. No, it doesn't. |
| Kitty | Why not? |
| **Gerald** | Because, secretly, I think I believe that maybe that's part of what your mother likes about me. We couldn't be more different. |
| Kitty | That's for sure! |
| **Gerald** | But along with being boring come one or two of the boring, old-fashioned virtues. |

| | |
|---|---|
| **Kitty** | Like what? |
| **Gerald** | Well, I think I can safely claim that I'm steady. I'm reliable. You can depend on me. And I'm predictable. At any time, you can be pretty sure where you can find me and what I will be doing. And that's not to be sneezed at. Maybe your mother likes that. Maybe she needs it. I know your sister does. |
| **Jude** | Do I? |
| **Gerald** | I think you do. |
| **Kitty** | I think she does, as well. |
| **Jude** | (*thoughtfully*) Yes, I suppose I do quite like you boring, Gerald. |

*Gerald bows gravely.*

| | |
|---|---|
| **Gerald** | I take that as a compliment, Judith. |

*He turns to Kitty.*

And I suppose I rather hoped that one day you might quite like me boring, too.

*There's a long pause. Then –*

| | |
|---|---|
| **Kitty** | Well, I suppose . . . Some day . . . I might . . . |
| **Gerald** | I hope so. |
| **Jude** | So do I. |

*There is another long pause. Then –*

| | |
|---|---|
| **Gerald** | Right! Everyone finished? Then it's time to wash up. Judith, it's your turn tonight. |
| **Jude** | (*outraged*) *My* turn? |
| **Gerald** | I think so, yes. Since Kitty did the dishes yesterday. |
| **Kitty** | (*bitterly*) And the day before. And the day before that. |
| **Jude** | (*to Kitty*) Well, you're a lot older than I am. |
| **Gerald** | That's quite irrelevant. Why, by that argument, the youngest child in every family would grow up incapable of clearing up after a meal. |
| **Jude** | But I'm so tired. |
| **Gerald** | So am I. And so is Kitty. |
| **Jude** | We could just leave the dishes till the morning. |

| | |
|---|---|
| **Gerald** | Only sluts and drunks leave the dishes till morning. |
| **Jude** | Mum *often* – |
| **Kitty** | Ju-ude! |

*Jude makes a face, but doesn't finish her sentence.*

| | |
|---|---|
| **Gerald** | Stop playing the baby, Judith. There's no point. Your mother may be soft as butter, but I'm not. I know as well as Kitty does that you're as capable as the next man of dipping your hands in the old Fairy Liquid and washing up the dishes. |

*Jude gives Gerald the evil eye. Kitty stares at him in admiration and wonder.*

Aren't you?

| | |
|---|---|
| **Jude** | (*sullenly*) I suppose so . . . |
| **Gerald** | There's my girl! And afterwards, as a reward, I'll come up and read to you. |
| **Jude** | Something good? |
| **Gerald** | Not half. |

*He takes a pamphlet from his pocket, and waves it temptingly in front of Jude, winking at her.*

| | |
|---|---|
| **Jude** | Oh, goody! That one! |

*Curious, Kitty reaches for the pamphlet. Gerald gives it up.*

| | |
|---|---|
| **Kitty** | (*reading*) 'The Ross and Killearn Step-by-Step Guide to Good Money Management . . .' |

*Kitty shakes her head at both of them.*

You guys are weird!

*Jude sniggers behind her hand, but Gerald acts hurt.*

| | |
|---|---|
| **Gerald** | But it has an extremely interesting chapter on the advantages of annual deferment in Earnings Related Pension Schemes. |
| **Jude** | It's my very favourite! |

*Kitty stares at them. Then, suddenly, she realizes that they're teasing her. She sets about them with the pamphlet.*

| | |
|---|---|
| **Kitty** | Jude! Gerald! |
| **Gerald** | (*laughing*) No! Stop it! I'm too old! Don't hurt me! |
| **Jude** | (*laughing*) Take it all back! Sorry, Kitty! Didn't mean it! |

*With all three of them laughing, Kitty beats Jude and Gerald out of the room.*


## Scene Six

*The living room.*

*Gerald comes in from Jude's bedroom, carrying the pamphlet and calling back over his shoulder. Kitty is on her way to bed.*

**Gerald**  And tomorrow night, Judith, we'll have the section on how higher rate taxpayers can get the very best from their savings.

*From offstage, sleepily.*

**Jude**  Night-night, Gerald.

*Gerald walks round, switching off all unnecessary lights.*

**Gerald**  There. That should slow the little electric wheel –

*He stops, remembering Kitty's essay. She grins at him from the doorway.*

(*reprovingly*) You shouldn't laugh, Kitty. The lights in this house probably keep two or three power stations from being made redundant. A smart recycling expert like you should be the first to –

**Kitty**  (*waving cheerily*) Nighty-night, Gerald.

**Gerald**  Night-night. Sleep well.

*Kitty goes off, yawning. Gerald yawns too. He settles on the sofa with Flossie and the paper. After a few moments of peace, he hears a bang at the door, a great rattle of the lock, and in bursts Mum.*

| | |
|---|---|
| **Mum** | Ta-ra! Ta-ra! I'm home! |
| | *She does a victory whoop and dance.* |
| **Gerald** | Rosalind! Please! Judith is fast asleep, and Kitty's just settling. Don't make so much noise. |
| | *Mum puts her hands on her hips.* |
| **Mum** | What sort of welcome is that for the conquering heroine? |
| **Gerald** | There's nothing at all heroic about waking two exhausted children. |
| **Mum** | You might have let them stay up till I got back! |
| **Gerald** | Kept them up, do you mean? Just to cheer you in? That's a bit self-indulgent, isn't it, when they have school in the morning. |
| | *Mum slings her small rucksack down on the floor.* |
| **Mum** | (*sourly*) Well, they'd have been a whole lot more welcoming than you. |
| **Gerald** | Naturally. They're a whole lot better brain-washed. |
| **Mum** | (*icily*) Brain-washed, Gerald? And brain-washed into *what*, may I ask? |
| | *Kitty appears in the doorway, unnoticed, in her nightie.* |
| **Gerald** | Into believing that what you're doing is more important than anything else. |
| | *Mum prises off her shoes.* |
| **Mum** | It is important, Gerald. |
| **Gerald** | Some people might say that getting yourself arrested on the spur of the moment is not so much important as irresponsible. |
| | *Mum hurls her shoes into the corner.* |
| **Mum** | And you'd be one of them, I suppose? |
| **Gerald** | Yes. Yes, I think I would. |
| **Mum** | Now, listen, Gerald. It's good of you to bring the girls home, and stay with them. I'm very grateful. But I'm not prepared to listen to abuse, and I don't take |

kindly to being called irresponsible by you. I am not irresponsible!

**Gerald** Oh, no?

**Mum** Oh, no! I think extremely hard before I take either of my children on anything like this. I don't take them anywhere things might get out of hand. And the first thing I did when I got to the station was insist on phoning Mrs Harrison. So don't you dare to call me irresponsible!

*Jude, wakened by raised voices, materializes at Kitty's side. Kitty puts an arm round her sister. Neither Gerald nor Mum notices.*

**Gerald** What would you call it, then?

**Mum** What would I call it? I'll tell you, Gerald. I would call it *anger*! I am *angry*, Gerald. More angry than you can imagine, or I can say. I am angry enough to leave home on a quiet Sunday morning. Angry enough to band together with people I don't even know. Angry enough to spend my only free time trying to save the only real inheritance any of us can offer to our children!

**Gerald** Now listen, Rosalind –

**Mum** Oh, no, Gerald! I won't listen! I won't listen to you! You are the enemy now! You, and people who think like you! People who are so stupid, so stubborn, so gullible, that they can go on ignoring the poisoned land on which they stand, the poisoned seas that surround them. Oh, go on, Gerald! Go on ignoring the billions of pounds wasted each year filling this planet with rubbish, and weapons, and chemicals that spoil things for longer than the factories will ever stand! Go on! Ignore the risks the power stations might explode, or leak worse than they do already! Keep on believing all the government experts, Gerald! You know they've lied to you again and again, but go on believing them anyway! And don't forget to ignore the generations of children forced to grow up fearing the very air they have to breathe!

**Gerald**   Rosalind –

**Mum**   No, Gerald! Don't come near me! Go on home! Go
home and put your head in a paper bag. Kitty's right!
You're just a goggle-eyes!

*Kitty is about to spring forward to Gerald's defence.
Jude tugs her back, and Kitty changes her mind.*

Go home and goggle away at your important share
prices. Goggle away at your pension payments and
your interest rates.

**Gerald**   Rosalind –

**Mum**   Don't for a moment think of acting irresponsibly! For
heaven's sake! Don't waste any of your precious,
precious time worrying about our little, frail, green
planet!

**Gerald**   Rosalind –

*Mum throws herself down on the sofa. Hiding her
face, she starts to sob. Gerald puts his hand on her
shoulder. Angrily, she shrugs it off.*

**Mum**   You don't care, do you? And you never will! So go
home, Gerald! Go home! And don't come back!

*He reaches out towards her again. Then he thinks
better of it. As Kitty and Jude silently watch him, he
reaches for his jacket, hesitates again, and then,
reluctantly, goes out of the door.*


## Scene Seven

*Downstairs.*

*Jude is entirely hidden behind an old newspaper.
Kitty is writing an essay at the table. Flossie is asleep
on a chair.*

**Jude**   (*hesitating over the words*) . . . and shares fell three –
no, *thirty*-three points down to one hundred – no,
one *thousand* – no, ten thousand?

**Kitty**   Why don't you give up, Jude? It's not as if you even really understand what any of it means.

**Jude**   I do!

**Kitty**   (*gently*) No, you don't. You just miss him, that's all.

**Jude**   No, I don't.

**Kitty**   Yes, you do.

**Jude**   Well, you miss him as well. I saw.

**Kitty**   Saw what?

**Jude**   The first page of that essay. When you went up to get another cartridge.

*Kitty automatically covers her essay.*

It's no use covering it up. I've seen it. You can't say you don't miss him too.

**Kitty**   Did you get another postcard this morning?

*Jude takes it out of her pocket.*

**Jude**   It looks exactly like Flossie.

*Kitty takes it and holds it up against Flossie. She makes a doubtful face.*

It does! I'm going to use it to make Flossie a passport.

**Kitty**   What did you do with that one he sent of the blackboard covered in hard maths?

**Jude**   Stuck it on my wall.

**Kitty**   Mum won't like that.

**Jude**   She's seen it.

**Kitty**   What did she say?

**Jude**   Nothing.

**Kitty**   Didn't she even take it down and read it?

**Jude**   No.

**Kitty**   Perhaps she didn't realize it was from Gerald.

**Jude**   I told her it was from him.

**Kitty**   What did she say?

**Jude**   She said: (*in a mystified voice*) 'Gerald?' As if I was
          talking about someone at school she'd never even
          heard of.

**Kitty**  (*angrily*) Isn't that typical! When she first started
          dragging Old Goggle-eyes round here every other
          night, she didn't even *notice* I hated his guts and
          wished him dead. Now that *she's* finished with him,
          he doesn't exist any more! You can go shooting to the
          doormat every morning to look for postcards –

**Jude**   I don't!

**Kitty**  Oh yes, you do. And you can sit struggling through
          some three-week-old stock market report. But does
          she let herself see it? No! Because it doesn't suit her.
          She's finished with him, so, for her convenience,
          we're supposed to finish with him too!

**Jude**   Maybe she thinks that you'd be glad he's gone.

**Kitty**  How would she know what I think? She never asks. In
          case the answer doesn't suit her!

          *Kitty bangs down her fist.*

          Parents have such a nerve! If they decide that things
          will be too complicated if you have feelings, then you
          don't have any feelings. Simple as that!

**Jude**   She misses him too. I saw her looking at the
          telephone.

**Kitty**  She obviously doesn't miss him enough to pick it up.

**Jude**   Maybe she will after today. After she's been to court
          and paid her fine, she might feel better.

**Kitty**  She isn't paying the fine.

**Jude**   I thought she had to. I thought that's why she had to
          go.

**Kitty**  If she pleads guilty and pays up like a good girl, she'll
          never get the chance to explain.

**Jude**   Explain?

**Kitty**  Why she did it. Beth says you only get to defend
          yourself if you insist you're not guilty. That way you
          get the chance to tell everyone why you did it. The

other way, you don't. That's why she's up there now, practising her speech. She's probably telling all the clothes in her wardrobe that (*imitating*) 'It is the citizen's right and duty to act by his or her conscience.'

**Jude**   Yesterday I heard her telling the spider plant in the bathroom that saying nothing was the same as saying yes.

**Kitty**   Beth told her that one! Silence implies consent! Beth says it will impress the legal eagles in the court.

**Jude**   It didn't impress the spider plant.

**Kitty**   (*anxiously*) I hope Beth knows what she's doing. She told her what to wear, as well.

**Jude**   What?

**Kitty**   Old-fashioned schoolmarm stuff. That suit she got for the divorce. Hair in a bun.

**Jude**   Yuk. Double yuk.

**Kitty**   (*scathingly*) Courtroom couture!

**Jude**   Sshh, Kitty! Here she comes!

**Mum**   (*from offstage, in speechifying tones*) And each day in this country, the number of acres of countryside lost to development –

*Mum enters, looking a fright in her suit with her hair scraped back. The children stare.*

Oh, God! What does it amount to? I can't have forgotten again!

*She notices Kitty and Jude staring.*

Well? How do I look?

*Jude makes an uneasy face, and shrugs.*

Kitty?

**Kitty**   I'm sure they'll think you're very respectable.

**Mum**   (*snappily*) Well, that *is* the point!

*She looks round, tense with nerves.*

God, this place is a tip! Perhaps, while I'm out, the two of you could tidy up a bit.

**Jude**  Will you be gone long?

**Mum**  I don't know, do I? I'm sure these things can take hours. But Mrs Harrison won't mind staying on.

**Kitty**  (*sarcastically*) Lucky old Mrs Harrison!

**Mum**  What is all this mess, anyway?

*Mum starts frenetically clearing up. Hastily, Jude folds her paper and sits on it. Kitty clutches her essay to her woolly.*

**Mum**  Can't either of you help?

**Jude**
**Kitty** } Sorry!

*They start tidying the things lying about.*

**Jude**  Is this yours, Kitty?

**Kitty**  Put this in your school bag, Jude.

**Mum**  Look at all this clutter!

*She spots something under the sofa.*

What's this?

*She pushes back the sofa. An unopened box of chocolates lies underneath.*

**Jude**  Gerald bought those. For you.

**Kitty**  On the way home from the demo.

**Jude**  He made the driver stop the bus so he could buy them.

**Kitty**  They'd cheer you up, he said, after a horrid morning on an ugly road site, and a horrid afternoon in a dingy police station.

*Mum stares at the chocolates. Then she tosses them in the waste-paper basket.*

**Mum**  If I can't have his support in the important things like my beliefs, I don't need the silly things like his chocolates.

**Kitty**   He might not care about the planet. That doesn't mean he doesn't care about you.

**Mum**   Why are you sticking up for him all of a sudden? You are the one who used to call him Goggle-eyes!

**Kitty**   Maybe I was. Things change.

**Mum**   They certainly do!

**Kitty**   (*steadily*) But some people are slower than others to notice. Slower to notice someone reading the same old business page in the same old paper for three whole weeks . . .

*Mum turns to stare at Jude. Catching sight of the paper, she tugs it from under Jude, inspects the date, and looks shocked.*

Slower to notice the same person hasn't gone up a set in maths, like Mrs Fairbrother almost promised.

*Mum covers her mouth in horror as she remembers.*

**Jude**   (*reproachfully*) Kitt-ee!

**Kitty**   It's true, though. Isn't it? He isn't there to explain it all over and over, and you've fallen behind again. Haven't you?

*Jude nods. Kitty turns to Mum.*

You've probably kidded yourself she misses the chocolates a little. Or the nice fizzy drinks. But it's Gerald she's missing. Isn't it?

*Jude nods.*

She misses the cuddles on the sofa. The bedtime reads. She probably even misses him making her do the washing up.

**Jude**   (*defensively*) It's just that I'd got used to him.

**Kitty**   And so had I.

*Mum looks as if the stuffing's been punched out of her.*

**Mum**   Maybe what he said about me that night was true. Maybe I am irresponsible.

**Kitty**   He said something else about himself that night. He said he thought that maybe he was too blind to see what we see. Too numb to feel what we feel. But he couldn't help it. He was born that way.

**Mum**   (*wonderingly*) Did he say that?

**Kitty**   Yes. Yes, he did.

**Mum**   Really?

*A thoughtful silence. It is broken by a car hoot outside.*

*From offstage.*

**Beth**   Rosie! Time to go!

*Mum hesitates, looking from one daughter to the other.*

**Mum**   I have to go. If I don't show up, I might go to jail.

**Jude**   (*panicked*) Mum!

**Kitty**   (*reprovingly*) Mum!

*Mum picks up her shoulder bag.*

**Mum**   Listen, you two. I'd no idea. None at all. We have a lot to talk about when I get back.

*There is another car hoot.*

Oh, Lord! My defence speech!

*She snatches up Kitty's essay.*

This isn't it!

*She catches sight of the title.*

'How Things Change.' Is this yours, Kitty?

*Mum's eyes travel down the first few lines. She gasps. Kitty bites her lip and looks away. Mum stares at her. Jude rushes up with Mum's speech notes.*

*From offstage.*

**Beth**   Rosie! Come *on*!

**Jude**   Here's your speech.

*Still staring at Kitty, Mum brushes the notes aside.*

**Mum**   No. I don't need them. I've just changed my mind. I'm going in there, pleading guilty straight away, paying the fine and coming home at once. At *once*. Mrs Harrison won't get to sit through a single soap opera.

*Kitty points up to the television room.*

**Kitty**   She's on her second already, you're so late leaving.

*Beth flings open the door.*

**Beth**   Rosie! Do you want to fetch up in jail for contempt?

**Jude**   Mum! Go now! Go on! Hurry! Quick!

**Mum**   I promise you – both of you – we'll sort it out.

*Mum reaches for Kitty.*

You do believe me, Kitty, don't you?

*Kitty has no time to answer. Beth and Jude are pushing Mum towards the door.*

**Jude**   Quick, Mum! You mustn't be late! You mustn't!

**Beth**   Step on it, Rosie!

*Beth and Jude push Mum through the door and follow her. Kitty stays behind.*

*From offstage.*

**Mum**   Wish me luck, Kitty!

**Kitty**   (*softly*) Bye, Mum. Good luck. And come home *soon*.


## Scene Eight

*Four hours later.*

*Jude is staring at the clock. Kitty is tapping her pencil nervously.*

**Jude**   Ten to two till ten to six. Five hours!

**Kitty**   Four.

**Jude**   Where is she? Why hasn't she come back?

**Kitty**   I don't know, do I?

**Jude** Maybe they've put her in jail!

**Kitty** No, Jude. They wouldn't do that. Not without – Not –
*She bites her lip.*

**Jude** You don't sound sure.

**Kitty** (*snapping*) Well, I'm not sure, am I? It's not
something that comes up all that often, wondering
whether the police will clap your mother in irons –
*Jude claps her hands over her ears.*
– without even telling you!
*Jude removes her hands.*

**Jude** Maybe they know that Mrs Harrison is here.

**Kitty** If they knew Mrs Harrison, they wouldn't think that
was going to do us very much good.
*From offstage, quavering.*

**Mrs Harrison** Kitty, dear! Could you bring me another cup of tea?

**Kitty** Coming, Mrs Harrison!

**Jude** Mum could be locked up. Now. They could be
stopping her from using a telephone. They can do
anything they like.

**Kitty** They can't do anything they like.

**Jude** How do you know?

**Kitty** Because Gerald told me he's twice written letters to
complain about the police's behaviour. And both
times he received a reply.

**Jude** Gerald? Complained about the police?

**Kitty** That's right.

**Jude** You would have thought . . .

**Kitty** I know. You'd think he'd be the sort to stick up for
them whatever. But it's not as simple as that. He says
it's important for them to remember who pays their
salaries and in whose name they hold their powers.
Once he complained about simple rudeness from a
traffic cop. And once he reported an officer for what
he called 'unnecessary use of force'.

**Jude**  What's that?

**Kitty**  Kicking a suspect when he's down.

*Jude's eyes light up.*

**Jude**  Phone him! Kitty! Phone him now!

**Kitty**  Mum would go spare.

**Jude**  I don't care. He could go round there. He could see what's happening.

**Kitty**  Jude, they're not even *speaking* to each other.

**Jude**  That doesn't matter! He can still look after her. He can still make sure she's all right.

**Kitty**  He'd say it was none of his business.

**Jude**  No, he wouldn't. Not Gerald. He never says it's not his business. He went on about your messy room, and you being paid for the potatoes. He sticks up for people being kicked in the street. He'd stick up for Mum. Gerald thinks *everything's* his business. That's why you couldn't stand him.

**Kitty**  You're right. That's why I couldn't stand him.

**Jude**  So phone him up! Quick! Where will he be? Home? In the office?

**Kitty**  He always said: 'At any time you can be pretty sure where you can find me and what I will be doing.'

*She looks at her watch.*

Five minutes to six! So he'll be still at work.

*Kitty riffles through the Yellow Pages.*

Printing and Photocopying Services. That's what we need. Where are you? Public Houses . . . Psychiatric Services . . . Stop sticking, pages!

**Jude**  I've got his number.

*She pulls a sheaf of postcards out of her pocket, and selects one.*

He said if ever I felt like ringing him . . .

*Kitty snatches the postcard, reads the number, and punches it out on the phone. Then she looks at her sister curiously.*

| Kitty | Have you? Have you ever rung him? Since? |
|---|---|
| Jude | I wanted to. I didn't think that Mum would like it. I thought – |

*Kitty turns her attention to the phone.*

**Kitty** Hello? Yes, yes please! Can I speak to Gera – To Mr Gerald Faulkner, please . . . What? Gone? But it's only five to six! . . . Oh, I see. (*thoughtfully*) Gone all afternoon . . . Gone ever since *when*, did you say?

*Her eyes light up.*

Quarter to two!

*She covers the mouthpiece and hisses to Jude.*

Wouldn't you just have *guessed* it?

*She uncovers the mouthpiece.*

Can I ask one more question, please? How far are you from the magistrates' court?

*She grins broadly.*

About ten minutes' walk. Just what I thought! No, thanks. No, I don't need anything else at all. Thank you. Goodbye.

*She replaces the receiver. She grins at Jude.*

Steady. Predictable. Reliable.

**Jude** You can depend on Gerald!

**Kitty** Boring, old-fashioned virtues!

*They swing one another round and round, singing.*

**Kitty** *"Reliable, steady and predictable!"*

**Jude** *"Boring and steady and reliable!"*

*The door flies open. In bursts Mum. Her hair is flying. She has flowers pinned all over the ghastly suit.*

**Mum** Ta-ra! Ta-ra! Enter the conquering heroine! Crack open the champagne!

*Kitty and Jude rush to hug her.*

**Kitty** Are you all right?

**Mum**     Of *course* I'm all right. I'm *better* than all right. I'm
         magnificent!

**Jude**    Why are you so excited? What happened?

**Mum**     I'll tell you what happened. I was wonderful! That's
         what happened.

**Kitty**   Were you acquitted?

**Mum**     Acquitted?

         *Mum looks blank.*

         No, I don't think I was acquitted. I think I was
         discharged. Yes. That's what I was. Discharged.

**Kitty**   What's the difference?

**Mum**     Oh, how should I know, Kitty? I'm not a lawyer. But
         maybe I should be. I made the best speech in the
         world.

**Kitty**   (*suspiciously*) How come you got to make a speech? I
         thought you told us you were going to plead guilty.

**Mum**     And so I was. But then I got a bit confused.

**Kitty**   That's not like you.

**Mum**     And pleaded the wrong way.

**Kitty**   Not like you at all.

**Mum**     (*blushing*) No.

**Kitty**   So why? Why did you get confused? Was there,
         perhaps, someone sitting in the court you were
         surprised to see?

**Mum**     You knew! You knew he'd be there! Honestly, Kits!
         You might have warned me! He practically startled
         me out of my wits! You've no idea what a shock it
         was to see him there glowering at me from in
         between all those people from Beth's church.

**Jude**    (*reproachfully*) You should be pleased he turned up.

**Mum**     Oh, yes. I am. Because, since he startled me into
         pleading not guilty, he got to hear my historic
         statement.

         *She stands on a chair.*

I said to them: 'It is *our* planet. And when we go to all the trouble and strain of raising our children properly, we want to know that there's a future for them. If we take time to prepare proper meals, and teach our children the names of all the animals and flowers, we want to know that they'll grow up, and the flowers and animals whose names they've learned will still be there for them!'

**Kitty** And was he listening?

**Mum** Who? The magistrate? It was a woman.

**Kitty** No, not the magistrate! Gerald! Was Gerald listening?

*Gerald has appeared in the doorway.*

**Gerald** Yes. I was listening. I was listening hard. I listened to the bit about children ending up in your hospital because of problems with the food they eat and the air they breathe. I heard the bit about not letting a few selfish, greedy people spoil the future for the rest of us. I listened when you said there's only so much effort and money to go round, and if it all goes into roads and weapon factories, it can't be spent on schools and hospitals. I listened to the end, when you said people can be pushed too far, and end up not loving the land they live in any more, or wanting to defend it, because it's too spoiled to love and no longer worth defending.

**Mum** And were you utterly convinced?

**Gerald** No. No, I wasn't.

*He takes her hand.*

But I do understand – I finally understand – how much it means to you. I'm sorry I was so insensitive. I'm sorry I treated something that is a most important part of you as if it were a silly fad, something that didn't really matter. I admire your commitment, and I wish that I was a little more like you.

*He shakes a warning finger.*

I'm *not*, mind. And I'm not going on any more demonstrations. Never again! But, if you'll let me,

|         |                                                                                                                                                       |
|---------|-------------------------------------------------------------------------------------------------------------------------------------------------------|
|         | Rosalind, I'll run off your fliers at the office, cheap. I'll give you good business advice. And, when you get home all cold and muddy, your supper will be waiting. |
| Mum     | It's very tempting, Gerald . . .                                                                                                                       |
| Gerald  | If you're arrested, I'll go round your friends to raise the bail money. And if you're sent down for criminal damage, I'll care for your girls till they let you out again. |
| Mum     | (*grinning*) What do you reckon, girls?                                                                                                                |

*Jude claps enthusiastically.*

| Jude   | Yes! Yes!                                   |
|--------|---------------------------------------------|
| Mum    | Kitty?                                       |
| Kitty  | (*wryly*) Anything to get rid of Mrs Harrison. |

*She claps her hand to her mouth.*

Oh, God! Her tea! I haven't taken her her tea!

*Gerald pulls a lemon from his pocket, and tosses it to Kitty.*

| Gerald  | While you're in the kitchen, Kitty . . . |
|---------|-------------------------------------------|
| Kitty   | Fizzy drinks! Yes!                        |

*Kitty goes to the kitchen. Jude is still staring ecstatically at Mum and Gerald hand in hand.*

| Gerald  | How about giving your sister a hand, Judith? |
|---------|-----------------------------------------------|
| Jude    | She'll be all right.                          |
| Gerald  | (*warningly*) Judith . . .                    |
| Jude    | Oh, OK.                                        |

*She leaves the room. Gerald turns to Mum.*

| Gerald  | So. Am I forgiven? Can we try again? |
|---------|---------------------------------------|

*Mum nods.*

| Mum     | I'm sorry, too. I was tired and grumpy that night. I was spoiling for a fight. And I've been very stubborn since, not ringing you. |
|---------|----------------------------------------------------------------------------------------------------------------------------------|
| Gerald  | I didn't ring you, either.                                                                                                         |
| Mum     | Shall we call it quits?                                                                                                            |

| | |
|---|---|
| **Gerald** | Yes, quits. |
| **Mum** | Quits. |

*Kitty and Jude's heads appear in the doorway, one above another. They are eavesdropping and spying.*

| | |
|---|---|
| **Mum** | Come and sit here. |

*She pats the sofa beside her.*

| | |
|---|---|
| **Gerald** | I'll just turn one or two of these lights off first. |

*Unseen by Gerald, Kitty rolls her eyes to heaven. Jude giggles. Gerald tours the room switching off unnecessary lights. The girls duck as he goes past.*

There. That should slow the little electric wheel down to a sprint!

*The girls both giggle. He switches off the light beside their door. Their faces vanish into darkness.*

Now, where were we?

*Now only one lamp is on. Gerald returns to the sofa. Tenderly, he leans forward to kiss Mum. Then, still gazing into her eyes, he reaches out a hand and switches off the last lamp. The stage is plunged into darkness. We hear giggles from the back. Then, from the side of the door to the television room, we hear a tremendous clattering, rattling of doorknob, crashing furniture, smashing ornaments. The stage remains in utter darkness.*

*Silence.*

*Then –*

| | |
|---|---|
| **Mrs Harrison** | (*a little plaintively*) Is my tea coming, dears? Or shall I make it for myself? |

*The End*

# QUESTIONS AND EXPLORATIONS

## 1 Keeping Track

### Act One: Scene One

1 The main character, Kitty, speaks directly to the audience to open the play. What effect does this have on the reader?

2 Why do you think Kitty's mother takes the phone into the hall?

3 When she says, 'Oh, goody! It *is* you', what tone of voice is she using?

4 When she gives the speech about her mother missing the meeting, what impression do you have of Kitty?

### Act One: Scene Two

1 Kitty instantly dislikes Gerald. Why? What does she do to show this?

2 Why does Kitty refer to her mother as a 'Barbie-doll'?

3 Gerald asks Kitty to explain why she goes to 'Protect the Planet' meetings. When he asks if it is to 'Get all the furry and feathery creatures out of their cages', what tone of voice is he using? What point is he trying to make?

4 Do you think Gerald is being reasonable during his argument with Kitty?

5 Much to Kitty's annoyance, Gerald prefers to call her mother Rosalind and her sister Judith, even though everyone else calls them Rosie and Jude. What does this show us about his personality and why does Kitty hate it so much?

6 Why does Kitty become so upset by the attention Gerald pays to her mother?

## Act One: Scene Three

1   What is your impression of Mrs Harrison?

2   List the ideas that Kitty has for killing Gerald. Do you think she would really like to murder him?

3   Why do you think Jude likes Gerald?

4   Look at Kitty's essay, 'Something I Hate'. What effect does her writing 'It' instead of 'He' have?

5   Judith cannot possibly be interested in hearing about the FT Share Index, so why does she beg Gerald to read it to her?

6   How do you imagine Gerald feels when he reads Kitty's essay and realizes that it's about him?

7   Why does he 'cover up' for Kitty by telling a joke and throwing the essay in the bin?

## Act One: Scene Four

1   Why does Kitty keep mentioning her father in front of Gerald?

2   Kitty's bedroom is a complete mess. Is her mother right simply to ignore it, or should there be rules ensuring that everyone accepts some responsibility for keeping the house relatively tidy?

3   Do you feel that Gerald is becoming too involved with the family's business? Kitty says, 'And he can't tell me how to be, or what to do! Because he's not my Dad!' Is she right?

## Act One: Scene Five

1   In what ways do both Jude and Kitty's bedrooms reflect their personalities?

2   Kitty doesn't seem to remember clearly what life was like when her father lived with them. What, according to Jude, was

the true situation? Why do you think there is a difference between Kitty's memories and the truth?

3   What does Kitty mean when she describes Gerald as a 'political Neanderthal'?

4   List all the reasons why it would be better if Gerald stayed with the family; then the reasons why it would be better if he did not.

## Act One: Scene Six

1   When Gerald criticizes her for charging her mother for the potatoes, how does Kitty feel? Write a diary extract showing her anger and frustration.

2   Kitty explains her position, Gerald explains his. Do you agree with either of them?

## Act Two: Scene One

1   Do you think Kitty is exaggerating Gerald's faults?

## Act Two: Scene Two

1   Kitty says, 'Whose feelings are supposed to count for most? Mine? Mum's? Or Jude's?' Do you feel sorry for Kitty? Or do you think she should try to get on with Gerald to please her mother and Jude?

## Act Two: Scene Three

1   Kitty tells Beth that Gerald is a visiting cousin. Why do you think she does this?

2   The banner seems to make more sense to Gerald than any arguments. Do you think the idea of putting dots to represent the millions of pounds spent on firepower is a good one? Give the reason for your answer.

**3** The 'snowballers' include a nun, an elderly lady and a middle-aged man. What is the effect of including these types of people among those willing to break the law?

**4** Jude refuses to hold the other end of Kitty's banner because 'It's too heavy for me.' What is your impression of Jude at the moment? Has your view of her changed at all over the course of the play?

**5** What is Mum's argument for allowing herself to be arrested at the expense of looking after Kitty and Jude? What is Gerald's argument against it? Which argument do you think is the most sensible?

**6** How does Gerald help Kitty cope with her mother being taken off to the police station?

## Act Two: Scene Five

**1** 'You really care about what things look like, don't you, Gerald? . . .'
'Yes. Yes, I think I do.'
Gerald believes that appearance is important: that if Kitty's group dressed 'like the professionals they are' people would take them more seriously. Is he right?

**2** The group shows its dissatisfaction with the road by protesting, going to jail, etc. Gerald feels that its time would be better spent writing letters to their MPs and the media. What do you think?

**3** Would you describe Gerald as 'boring'?

**4** Kitty's opinion of Gerald seems to be softening. Why do you think this is?

**5** Gerald tells Jude to 'stop playing the baby'. Do you think that this is what she has been doing?

## Act Two: Scene Six

1   Is Gerald fair when he describes what Mum has done as 'not so much important as irresponsible?'

2   Make a list of the things Mum talks of in her long speech. Is she fair here to send Gerald home to 'goggle away at your important share prices'?

## Act Two: Scene Seven

1   Why is Jude continuing to read three-week-old business pages?

2   'She's finished with him, so, for her convenience, we're supposed to finish with him too!'
    Do you think parents should take their children's feelings into account when dealing with their own adult relationships? Do you think it is possible for them to do so?

3   'How Things Change.' We don't find out what Kitty writes in her essay. What do you think it might be?

## Act Two: Scene Eight

1   Why is Mum so exhilarated when she returns from the court?

2   What has Gerald learned about Mum?

3   This last scene is very dramatic and the mood of the scene changes quickly. What is the mood of the scene when:
    **a)** Kitty and Jude think their mother may have been arrested?
    **b)** Mum enters?
    **c)** Gerald enters?
    **d)** Mum and Gerald sit together?
    Do you think Mrs Harrison's humorous entrance at the end works well?

# 2 Explorations

## Characters

1 At times during the play Kitty addresses the audience directly to tell us what she thinks of 'Goggle-eyes'. However, we aren't always told her innermost thoughts and feelings.

Write diary entries for Kitty at the following points:

a *After Act One, Scene Two*. What does Kitty think about Gerald at this point? What are her thoughts about her own behaviour? Is she embarrassed or pleased by her outburst?

b *After Act One, Scene Six*. How does Kitty feel about Gerald interfering in her arrangement for digging the potatoes? How does she feel about having upset her mother? How does she feel about herself?

c *After Act Two, Scene Four*. How does Kitty feel about Gerald now? How have her feelings towards him changed? How does she feel about herself?

2 We don't hear what is in Kitty's essay, 'How Things Change.' However, we can guess much of what is in it. Write Kitty's essay.

3 Imagine Jude did contact Gerald during the time he and her mother weren't speaking to each other. Write Jude's letter to Gerald telling him what the house is like without him and why she is missing him.

4 At the beginning of the play Kitty addresses the audience directly to tell them her thoughts about her parents splitting up. Imagine Gerald has the chance to address the audience directly at the end of Act One. Write the speech in which he tells the audience his opinions of and feelings about Kitty and Jude.

5  In Act One it is clear that Kitty often misses her father and very clear that she can't stand 'Goggle-eyes'. Imagine that at some point in Act One she writes to a teenage magazine problem page outlining her problems and frustrations. Write both Kitty's letter and the reply from the magazine.

## Drama

1  Work in groups of five or more. Decide who will play the characters of Kitty, Jude, Mum and Gerald.

a) Play Act One, Scene Three from the point Kitty says, 'Well, I don't like Goggle-eyes. Not one bit.' to just before Gerald says to Mum, 'You missed a joke.'

b) At this point the extra person(s) should mould the characters into a position that most effectively shows the attitude each character and what is happening in the scene.

c) When everyone is 'frozen' the spare person(s) touch(es) each of the characters on the shoulder. The characters must then explain exactly how they are feeling.

d) Repeat the exercise using other scenes in which all four characters are present (for example, the end of Act One, Scene Two).

2  Anne Fine gives us a description of the characters at the beginning of the play. Throughout the play she also often tells us what the characters are wearing. However, there is still a lot of scope to play the characters in different ways.

Imagine you are going to direct a production of *Goggle-Eyes*. Write notes to tell an actor how you want the character of Gerald to be played. Consider the following questions before writing your notes:

a) How should Gerald speak? Should he have a regional accent?

**b)** When Gerald is arguing with Kitty should he raise his voice or should he remain calm and patient?

**c)** Should Gerald be seen as a slightly comic character or as a serious character?

**d)** Are there any other points you think would be useful for the actor?

## From Novel to Play

1 *Goggle-Eyes* was originally written as a novel. If you have enjoyed the play you will probably enjoy reading the novel too. (It is available in Puffin.)

In the novel Kitty tells the 'story' of Goggle-eyes to Helen in the cloakroom. Kitty's story is told in flashbacks. Why do you think Anne Fine chose not to use this structure in the play?

2 Choose a particular scene from the play and find the same section in the novel. For example, Act One, Scene Two (pp. 20–31 of the novel); Act Two, Scene Five (pp. 102–115 of the novel).

**a)** What changes did Anne Fine make to the scene to adapt it for the stage?

**b)** Do you think the scene works best in novel form or in play form?

## Debate: Rights and Responsibilities

1 Gerald describes Kitty's bedroom as a 'pit':

'Blackened banana skins. Shrivelled apple cores. Clothes all over, coated in cat hairs. Half-empty cups of stone-cold coffee, growing mould . . . Make-up spilling out on the dressing table. Pens leaking on the rug. Crumpled-up papers everywhere. Blouses and underwear fighting their way out of the drawers.'

At times Gerald really nags Kitty as he feels she has a responsibility to keep her room tidy.

Discuss what responsibilities you think children should have.

a) All children have rights as well as responsibilities. What rights do you feel children should have?

b) Design two posters. One shows 'Children's Rights'; the other shows 'Children's Responsibilities'.

2 'It is the citizen's right and duty to act by his of her conscience.'

a) Kitty's mother believes it is her *right* to protest against the new car-park however she can, even if she breaks the law. Do you agree with her?

Demonstrators calling for improved standards for animals being carried from the UK to Europe for slaughter have ended up in conflict with the police. Debate in class whether you think they were right to go this far in pressing for the cause that they believed in.

Alternatively, debate this question in relation to any other current issue which has provoked unlawful behaviour among its supporters.

b) Kitty's mother also believes that it is her *duty* to protest against damage to the countyside. She believes in preserving the world for future generations.

In what ways do you feel we have a duty to the world we live in? Discuss how far you would go to protect our natural environment – would you avoid dumping litter, recycle bottles, pay more for environmentally friendly products, go on a demonstation?

## Planning a Campaign

1 Kitty and her mother care about environmental issues and are involved in various campaigns: they care about protecting the

planet from nuclear weapons and pollution, protecting the countryside from road-building, and protecting animals against cruelty.

a) Make a list of other issues people feel strongly about.

b) Use your library to find out about: The Campaign for Nuclear Disarmament; Greenpeace; Friends of the Earth; Compassion in World Farming.

2 In groups, you are going to plan your own campaign against something you feel strongly about.

a) First decide on an issue which makes you concerned or angry. Research the issue thoroughly. You may wish to write to the groups listed above or to groups concerned with your particular issue for more information.

b) Next plan a strategy for your campaign. You might want to use: posters, advertisements in magazines/newspapers, letters to newspapers, speeches on television or radio, petitions for people to sign.

Decide how many of these methods you will use and in what order. Write down what you have decided – this is your campaign strategy.

c) Decide who will be responsible for each part of the campaign. Design the posters, write the advertisements, etc.

d) Prepare a presentation of your campaign for the rest of the class. Decide who will be responsible for each part of the presentation and practise it before you present it to the class.

# GLOSSARY